Softly in the Night

KENDELL FOSTER CROSSEN
Writing as
M.E. CHABER

STEEGER BOOKS / **2020**

PUBLISHED BY STEEGER BOOKS
Visit steegerbooks.com for more books like this.

PUBLISHING HISTORY

Hardcover
New York: Holt, Rinehart & Winston (A Rinehart Suspense Novel), February 1963. Dust jacket by Ben Feder, Inc.
Toronto: Holt, Rinehart & Winston of Canada, 1963.
London: T.V. Boardman (American Bloodhound Mystery #433), 1963. Dust jacket by Denis McLoughlin.

Paperback
New York: Paperback Library (63-288), A Milo March Mystery, #6, March 1970. Cover by Robert McGinnis.

ISBN: 978-1-61827-528-8

For Lisa, who shares everything that belongs to me except my heart; that she has completely.

CONTENTS

ONE

I read about it in the newspaper without realizing it was any more to me than just another story. I was in my office on Madison Avenue one Tuesday morning, reading the *New York Times*. I didn't have any work at the moment, so I was reading it from cover to cover. The item was on one of the back pages. A large beach house had burned in Santa Monica, California, on Sunday night. The firemen had managed to keep the fire from spreading, but the house had been completely destroyed. When the embers were searched later, two bodies were found. It was believed that the bodies were those of a Richard Cantwell and his wife. Cantwell was a wealthy Los Angeles businessman who owned the house that had burned. That was all.

As I turned to the sports page, the phone rang. I picked up the receiver and said hello.

"Milo, boy, how are you?" It was Martin Raymond, a vice-president of Intercontinental Insurance.

"All right, I guess," I said. "I haven't checked recently."

"Feel like running up here?" he asked. "I think I might have a little something for you."

"Sure," I said. "I'll be right there." I hung up and folded the newspaper. The sports would have to wait. This probably meant a job, and I could use one.

I'm Milo March. March's Insurance Service Corporation. I'm the whole corporation. I'm an insurance investigator.

I walked up Madison Avenue to the Intercontinental Building. Raymond's office was on the executive floor where they really let themselves go on furnishings, from carpeting with ankle-deep nap to receptionists with wrist-deep measurements. The redhead at the desk was a good example. I admired her while she found out that it was all right for me to go into the inner sanctum. I took a last, loving look and waded back to Raymond's private office. He was waiting for me.

"Milo, boy," he said. Everybody was a boy to him. "Glad you could make it."

"It was a little rough on the back slope," I said, "but the dogs mushed on through."

He gave an executive-type laugh. "That's my boy, always pushing the old laugh meter. Feel like taking on a little job?"

"That depends on how little," I said. "If it's less than a day I don't think I can spare the time."

"It'll be several days," he said. "A suspected arson case out in California. Santa Monica."

I remembered the morning newspaper. "It wouldn't be the Cantwell fire, would it?"

He looked surprised. "You know about the case?"

"Only what I read in the paper this morning. A beach house burned down in Santa Monica and there were two bodies found in the ruins. Believed to be the remains of Mr. and Mrs. Cantwell. Is that the case?"

He nodded. "That's it."

"The newspaper didn't say anything about arson."

"It wouldn't," he said. "In fact, we're the only ones who think it was arson. The local police and fire departments have already stated that the fire was of unknown origin. The newspaper probably got its story from them."

" 'Everybody's queer but me and thee,' " I quoted. "How did you arrive at the conclusion that everyone is wrong except the company that has to pay for the fire?"

"Listen," he said, "Richard Cantwell had that house insured for three hundred thousand dollars. He owned another house in Beverly Hills, which we insured for three hundred and fifty thousand dollars. We carry all of the insurance on his business—insurance on the building in Los Angeles, embezzlement and theft insurance, accident insurance on his employees."

"That hardly seems reason enough to think that the man had his own house set on fire."

"That's not all," he said dryly. "We also carried life insurance on Richard Cantwell and on his wife. Two hundred and fifty thousand on each. Double indemnity. Which means a half million on each if the death is accidental. So if that was Cantwell and his wife in the fire, we owe one million three hundred thousand dollars—to start with."

"What does that mean?" I asked.

"Three weeks ago," he said, "we received an anonymous letter accusing Richard Cantwell of embezzling from his own company. The writer of the letter thought that we would be interested, since we had the company insured. We didn't pay too much attention to the letter at the time, because it wasn't signed. We did turn it over to our Los Angeles office. They made a quick check and said there was no evidence of anything wrong in Cantwell's company. So we dropped it."

"Now you want to pick it up again?"

"It might be worth looking into," he said. "We don't like the looks of it, Milo. There are too many coincidences and I don't believe in them. He has embezzlement insurance and somebody says he's dipping into the cash. He has insurance on a beach house and it burns down. He has insurance on himself and his wife—paying double in case of accident—and then we are told that he and his wife died in the fire."

"Who collects?"

"That's what we're going to pay you to find out," he said. "I can think of several possibilities. Maybe somebody was helping him dip into the company cash; maybe somebody had an eye on those two insurance policies for some time. It might even have been Cantwell himself."

"You have a nasty mind," I said.

"It's been known to happen."

"True," I admitted. "I've worked on some like that. Do you have anything else that points to arson?"

"Not really, but there is something else that I think might fit. We make a practice of keeping track of most of the professional arsonists. There is one man here in New York we believe to be working on a large scale. We believe that he and his organization are responsible for more than a hundred fires in the Greater New York Area in the past year. And we feel sure that he doesn't confine his work to this area. But we haven't been able to pin anything on him yet."

"Why not?" I interjected.

"Too big and too good an organization. It's like asking why the cops don't clean up all the bookies or policy men. We've managed to catch several of his men and send them to prison, but none of them has talked, and there has been no way to tie them into the ring. Yet we're positive that it's operating, and we think it may be active in more than just arson."

"What do you mean?"

"A little more than a year ago we paid a policy on an accidental death claim. We think the man was murdered, but we've never been able to prove it. But we do know that when the beneficiary collected the money, she immediately withdrew half of it in cash, and that there were no signs of her making any special purchases. We believe she split the money with the gang."

"Maybe she just likes to keep a few bills tucked away in the mattress," I suggested.

"Maybe," he said without belief. "Anyway, we have quite a file on this gang, but it's all guesswork and all on other cases. You can look it over if you like, but I doubt that it will help on this one. What I started out to tell you was that about a week ago one of our men got a tip that four of the ring's best men had left town on a big job. But that was all he could get. He hasn't even been able to find out which four men went. We do know, however, that the head of the ring is in Southern California, supposedly on vacation. This was a big enough job, so he might have gone there to supervise it personally."

"Sounds possible," I said. "Who's the head of the ring?

"Harry Manfred. Ever hear of him?"

"Sure," I said. "Who hasn't? He's one of the old racket boys who's way up on top in the Syndicate. It's a long time since he's been investigated by anybody below the Federal cops."

"Well, that's what I think we're up against. We haven't been able to make any headway against Manfred or his gang in the other cases. Unless you can do something now, this one is going to cost us at least one million three hundred thousand dollars."

"It's only money," I told him. He winced, as I knew he would. "I'll do my best, Martin. I can probably track down the men who did the job, but getting anything on Manfred himself may be another story. Better men than I have tried that and come out second best."

"I know," he said gloomily. "But we know that you're the best man we can get on the job."

"Thanks," I said. "By the way, who is the beneficiary on the two life insurance policies?"

"Mrs. Cantwell was the beneficiary on her husband's policy and he was on hers."

"And who gets the million dollars if it is both Cantwells in the fire?"

"Some foundation for improving the ties between the East and the West. It also gets the fire insurance money if both the Cantwells are dead."

"You mean that cultural foundations are hiring arsonists these days?" I said. "What is the world coming to?"

He gave me a dirty look. "For a million dollars, anyone will do anything. You should know that."

"Aren't we the suspicious ones?" I said. "It's a good thing

they have electric razors. Sometimes I think I might not trust myself to shave my own throat. Got anything else on the case?"

"Not much. When you get to California, go to our Beverly Hills office. They'll have a file made up for you, but there won't be too much in it. And get there as soon as you can."

"The first Pony Express that leaves," I promised. "That's all?"

"My secretary has some expense money for you and I've authorized the Beverly Hills office to give you more if you need it. Oh, yes, we will see to it that you get a healthy bonus if you manage to wrap this up."

"Now you're playing our song," I said. "Well, I'll see you around, Martin."

"Keep in touch. And good luck, Milo."

I went out and his secretary handed me an envelope that was fat with bills. As I went down the corridor, I opened it and did a quick inventory. There was two thousand dollars in the envelope. I whistled to myself. If Martin Raymond, who usually screamed like a wounded bull over every dollar of expense money, was starting me off with two thousand, it showed how badly they wanted the case solved.

I went back to my office and told my telephone answering service that I'd be out of town for an indefinite period. I called the airlines and made a reservation for Los Angeles. They put me on a jet flight leaving at midnight. So on the way downtown I stopped and picked up the ticket.

I have an apartment on Perry Street down in the Village. I stopped off there and got everything packed for the trip. That still left the afternoon and half the night. I went over to the Blue Mill, had two martinis and some lunch, and talked to Alcino for a while. That killed a couple of hours. I used up the rest of the afternoon doing a little quiet pub crawling and then went to Adamo's on Minetta Lane. I talked with Freddy and Tony while I had a couple of martinis and then I had dinner. I wasted enough time over coffee and brandy so that when I got back to my apartment it was time to leave for the airport.

I slept most of the way to Los Angeles. Due to the speed of the jet and the time difference, it wasn't much later when we landed than it had been when we took off from New York. I took a cab to Santa Monica and registered in the best hotel. I had a couple of drinks in the bar and went to bed.

I was up early the next morning and went down to the Beverly Hills office of Intercontinental. I wound up with a man who was a road-company edition of Martin Raymond. His name was Norbett. He gave me the Cantwell folder and an office to work in.

Martin Raymond had been right. There wasn't much in it. There was the original report from the time the investigation for the policies was made. It didn't give too much. Cantwell was fifty-two; his wife was thirty. He had been a successful businessman for more than twenty years, operating an export-import company. The investigator had stated that he believed Cantwell was keeping one or two mistresses, but the company had apparently believed that he was still moral enough to have the policy. It was true that there was nothing else to make him look like a bad risk.

Copies of the policies were also in the file. They were the

usual standard policies, but I did notice one interesting thing. Cantwell owned a house in Beverly Hills and another one up in the mountains, in addition to the one in Santa Monica that had burned down. The two remaining houses were not insured for their full value. That could mean that Cantwell had planned on burning the beach house, since it was insured to the hilt.

There were also copies of police and fire reports. They agreed that the fire was of unknown origin. The police had identified the two bodies in the fire as being those of Richard and Pamela Cantwell. Neither identification was very firm, although one report said that Richard Cantwell had been identified through his dental work. The bodies had been almost completely destroyed.

I made a note of the name of the cop in charge of the investigation, a Lieutenant Frank Arnold, and left the file on the desk. I went down and took a cab to the police station.

I had to wait a few minutes and then was shown into Lieutenant Arnold's office. He was a big, gray-haired man who looked as if he would have been happier on a beat than behind a desk. He looked at my identification and then passed it back to me.

"I wondered when one of your people was going to show up," he said. "There's a lot of money riding on the Cantwells, and I figured that the company wouldn't be satisfied with the official work."

"Well, we have a small interest in it," I said with a smile. "That doesn't mean that we're automatically dissatisfied with the official work. It's just that sometimes we have made time to fool around with the case—in cooperation with the police, of course."

"Of course," he said amiably. "I got nothing against private and insurance dicks. I even like them—when they cooperate with us. Know what I mean?"

"Sure," I said. "I go along with that. Take me, I like cops—when they cooperate with me."

He laughed. "All right, March. We understand each other. What can I do for you?"

"Tell me about the Cantwell case."

"Somebody put the torch to the house," he said. "We know that now. We found traces of gasoline. Oh, it was a professional job all right, but you can't completely conceal those things. We've checked out all the local professionals and we don't think any of them did it. We think it was imported talent. But we don't know who the talent is or who imported it—yet. We'll find out."

"I've heard that some men from New York might have been sent here," I said, "and that the man they work for is also here."

"You mean Harry Manfred?" he asked.

"You know about him?"

"Every cop knows about Harry Manfred," he said. "We've heard that Manfred may be involved in arson now, so we looked around. There's nothing to connect him with Cantwell or the fire, and so far we haven't found any evidence that any of his men are here. We'll keep on looking."

"I'm sure you will," I said. "I'll do a little looking myself, if you don't mind."

"I don't mind—as long as you don't get in the way."

"I never get in the way," I said. "I keep on the move. What do you know about this foundation that's named as second beneficiary in the insurance policies?"

"It's a non-profit-making corporation headed by a girl named Kayoko Asakura."

"Japanese?"

"Yes, but a third-generation American citizen. So far as our records show, it's a legitimate foundation. It's been in existence for about three years."

"Money?"

"It gets money in and spends it. Very little of it goes for overhead. I believe that Cantwell was one of the heavy contributors."

"Why?"

"Who knows. Cantwell did a lot of business with Japan, so maybe that was the reason. Why are you interested in it?"

"It's obvious," I said. "With Mr. and Mrs. Cantwell both dead, the foundation gets more than a million dollars."

"That's true," he said. He smiled. "It'll be in the papers later. Mrs. Cantwell isn't dead."

TWO

It took a few minutes for that to sink in. I had so thoroughly accepted the idea that both of them were dead that I wasn't sure of what I was hearing. But it finally penetrated, and I looked at Arnold. He was enjoying the situation.

"But," I said, "I thought that both bodies were almost completely destroyed."

"They were," he said. "The woman wasn't Mrs. Cantwell. She was up at their place in the mountains for several days. No radio, no television, and no newspapers, so she didn't know anything about it until she came back to the city late yesterday. She was quite broken up about it."

"I'll bet," I said. "She's worth at least eight hundred thousand more than she was when she went up to the mountains. Was she up there alone?"

He made a clucking sound with his tongue. "That's the trouble with you insurance fellows; you're suspicious of everybody. No, she wasn't alone. She had a friend with her. A female friend."

"How jolly," I said. I was feeling irritable because the picture had suddenly changed. I always reacted that way for a few seconds until I had a chance to adjust to the new picture. "What were they doing up there, holding hands?"

"You do get nasty, don't you?" he said with a smile. He was

still enjoying himself. "We've already talked to Mrs. Cantwell and her friend and double-checked their story. It stands up."

"Okay," I said. "So Mrs. Cantwell is alive. Then who's the woman in the fire?"

"I don't know," he said. "There wasn't much to go on. We weren't sure at the time that it was Mrs. Cantwell. It was a woman of about her age and size. She had perfect teeth—as does Mrs. Cantwell—so we couldn't get a dental identification. We were guessing in the beginning. Now we don't have any guesses."

"Were you guessing on Cantwell, too?"

"Not so much. There wasn't any more to go on except that the teeth checked out with Cantwell's dental records."

"All right," I said. "Where does this leave us? You say that somebody set the fire. So the same somebody must have wanted to get Cantwell and the unnamed woman, not to mention a few hundred thousand dollars. Who? Mrs. Cantwell? She does the collecting. Or is Cantwell's body a ringer, and he's waiting in the wings for her to get the check?"

"There are several possibilities," he agreed. "We've thought of all of them, I guess. It might be Mrs. Cantwell even though she was away when it happened. It could be Cantwell himself who found a ringer, as you suggest. It's also possible that someone with a grudge against Cantwell decided to burn down his house and Cantwell and his friend were accidentally trapped in the fire. Your company won't like that version, but it's possible."

"It's possible," I said, "but I'll tell you something. It's very seldom that a man insured for that much really dies accidentally. I'll believe it when I see one."

"We'll work on all the possibilities," he said.

"I'm sure you will. Could you tell where the two bodies were when the fire got them?"

"The bedroom."

"Any signs that they'd been knocked out before the fire?"

"No."

"Any evidence that they'd been trying to get out of the building?"

He shook his head. "They could have been overcome by smoke while still asleep. It happened at two in the morning."

"What does Mrs. Cantwell say about the possible identity of the woman in the fire?"

"She doesn't. I gather that she knew that he played around whenever he had the chance, but she had never bothered to find out who any of the women were."

"How are you doing on that score?"

"Not so good," he admitted. "Oh, we've dug up the names of some of the girls he went out with, but none of them are missing. If the girl in the fire was a date, she must have been a new one."

"Whoever she is," I said, "she is certainly missing, and you'd think somebody would connect her with Cantwell."

"If they do we'll find out about it," he said.

I began to get an idea about him. He was going to go on being friendly, answering all my questions, but he wasn't going to give me very much. There'd never be anything I could complain about, and that's the way it would go with him until the case was over.

"Well," I said, "I don't want to sit around wasting the

taxpayers' money. You probably have a lot of things to do, and I wouldn't want to interfere."

"Of course not," he said amiably. "I suppose you'll be around for a while, reading all the reports and that sort of thing?"

I returned his smile. "I expect so. I may even write a few reports myself."

"Good. I always like to see civic-minded citizens who like to help the police. I'll be looking forward to seeing any ideas that you have, March."

"Speaking of reports," I said, "I don't suppose I could see the complete reports you have on the case so far?"

"I'm afraid not." He sounded as if he really regretted it. "Department rules, you know. But I'll be glad to tell you anything you want to know. I told you I always like to cooperate."

"I've noticed," I said evenly. "Well, some other time, Lieutenant." I headed for the door.

"Anytime, March. Where you headed for now?" He tried to make the question sound casual, but it didn't quite come off.

"With the company losing so much money," I said solemnly, "I may just go back to the hotel and have a good cry. After that I may think of something. Good-bye, Lieutenant." I closed the door gently behind me and went on out of the station house.

One thing was clear. I was going to have to do all my own digging, which was about par for the course. I figured I had at least one good place to start. I took a taxi to Hollywood and rented a car. Since Martin Raymond was being so generous with expense money, I made it a Cadillac. There was no point in feeling underprivileged while I was trying to save his million dollars.

I drove out to Beverly Hills and found the Cantwell home without any trouble. It was a big, imposing house with enough land around it to start a housing project. I parked in the driveway and went up to the front door. A maid answered when I rang the bell.

"Mrs. Cantwell," I said.

"I'm sorry," the maid said, "Mrs. Cantwell isn't seeing anyone today. There's been a terrible tragedy in the family and she's in mourning."

"I know," I said. "You run along and tell her that it's Mr. March from the insurance company, and I think perhaps she'll see me."

She looked doubtful as she closed the door and left me waiting. She was back in a few minutes and this time she looked surprised.

"She'll see you for a few minutes," she said. "Please follow me."

That wasn't difficult to do. Her uniform was tight and she had a nice walk, especially going up the stairs. We reached the second floor and she led the way to the back of the house. She opened the door and stood to one side.

"Mr. March is here, Mrs. Cantwell," she said.

I stepped inside the room and got my first look at the widow. It was quite a sight. She was tall and blond with hair that fell down over her shoulders like spilled wheat. On the record she was thirty years old, but she didn't look a bit more than twenty-five. She wore a red dress that clung to her body with loving care—and I didn't blame it. When my gaze finally lifted to meet hers there was a knowing smile on her face.

"Mr. March?" she said. "I understand that you wanted to see me." There was just a slight emphasis on the word *see*. It might have been an accident, but I thought otherwise.

"I had some thoughts about it," I said. "That is, if you're Mrs. Cantwell."

"I'm Pamela Cantwell," she said. "You look as if you doubted it, Mr. March."

"I don't doubt it," I said. "I'm just a little surprised. I was expecting something more along the lines of a conventional widow. You know, the mourning clothes, the weeping eyes— that sort of thing."

She laughed softly. "Are you always so naive, Mr. March?"

"Maybe. But I understood that you only learned about your husband's death yesterday."

"That is quite true. I was married to Richard Cantwell, Mr. March. I suppose I was in love with him when I married him, but a lot of things have happened since then. For the past five years we had what might be called an arrangement. Richard went his way and I went mine. It pleased both of us. I am sorry that Richard was killed—as sorry as I would be to learn that any human was killed—but that is all. For me to put on widow's weeds would be nothing but a mockery. Does that explain my red dress, Mr. March?"

"I suppose so," I said. "Give me a little time; I'll probably get used to it. In the meantime, I'd like to ask you a few questions."

"Why?"

"Eight hundred thousand reasons. Each one of them a dollar. That is how much my company is supposed to pay for the death of your husband and the burning of your house. Insurance companies are very peculiar, Mrs. Cantwell. They don't like it when somebody puts a match to property they've insured and in the process also accidentally kills a man who carries a double-indemnity policy."

"But I would think they would be delighted," she said. "I understand that everyone originally believed that I had died in the fire with Richard. That would have cost your company one million three hundred thousand dollars. So you see, you have already saved five hundred thousand dollars."

"We appreciate every dollar of it," I said dryly, "but we still have a certain amount of interest in the rest of it."

"I don't see how you can possibly contest the claims," she said. "I've already spoken to my attorney. He says there's no question about it. The house did burn down and it was insured against fire. My husband did die accidentally in the fire. His life was also insured. So there's nothing to contest, is there, Mr. March?"

"I don't remember saying anything about contesting the claims, Mrs. Cantwell. I only mentioned asking a few questions."

She stared at me for a minute, then her face softened and she laughed. "I'm sorry. I guess I'm more on edge than I realized. Too much has happened too quickly. I came back just yesterday and learned about Richard. Then I answered all the questions for the police. I'm afraid I've been rude, Mr. March. Please forgive me. I'll answer all of your questions, of course. Won't you sit down?"

"Thank you," I said. I took the nearest chair.

"May I get you a drink?" she asked.

"Why not? When I was very young, my father told me never to say no to a drink or a beautiful woman."

She smiled. "What will you have, Mr. March?"

"V.O., if you have it. On the rocks."

She went over to a small portable bar and made two drinks. She came across the room and handed one to me. "Go ahead, Mr. March. What would you like to know?"

"I won't give you too much trouble, Mrs. Cantwell," I said. "Tell me, do you think that was really your husband who died in that fire?"

She looked surprised. "The police said it was. They said they had managed to identify the—the body."

"They also identified the other body as being yours."

"Yes, but they said the identification of Richard was more certain. What are you trying to say, Mr. March?"

"It is just barely possible," I said gently, "that your husband planned the whole thing and thoughtfully provided a substitute corpse for himself."

"But the money comes to me."

"True. Which opens up two possibilities. You and your husband might have agreed upon a plan that gives the money to you and then you join him later, when it seems safe. Or maybe he didn't tell you about it, and intends to surprise you later by showing up and demanding his share."

"Why should my husband do anything like that? He was a wealthy man."

"Maybe. He used to be, but maybe he wasn't so wealthy recently. Was he?"

"So far as I know. We certainly hadn't changed our way of living." She looked at me curiously. "Doesn't it even occur to you that my husband's death might have been the accident that it appears to have been?"

"It's occurred to me—but it still was arson. There is no question that the fire was deliberately set."

"Couldn't that have been arranged by someone who was an enemy of Richard's? Maybe by someone who didn't know he was in the house, but just wanted to destroy our property out of spite?"

"It's possible," I admitted, "but it's not the only possibility. Did you have any particular enemy in mind when you mentioned that?"

"Richard made many enemies. He was not a very friendly man."

"Do you mean in business?"

"Both in business and socially."

"Who are those enemies?"

"I don't know," she said with a shrug. "I only know that Richard was always fighting with someone. Perhaps they could tell you at the office."

"I intend to check with them," I said. "You know, there is something that I'm very curious about. The woman whose body was found with your husband's. Any idea who she was?"

"No. Richard was interested in many women. I don't suppose any of them lasted very long. I didn't bother trying to keep up with who was current."

"You didn't care?"

"Not in the slightest."

"Could it have been a jealous husband out to get his wife and her lover?"

"I suppose it could have been. I imagine there were jealous husbands in Richard's life."

"Who would have known about the women in his life?"

"I haven't the vaguest idea. Richard had no friends, if that's what you had in mind. Perhaps someone at the office might know. Or try the headwaiters in the various restaurants and clubs. But, whatever you find, it should prove one thing to you."

"What?"

"That it was Richard in the fire. If he'd been planning it, there wouldn't have been any point to killing the woman."

"There might have been," I said. "I can think of two ways where there might have been a point to it. You were out of town. Maybe he picked someone who would be mistaken for you, with the idea of also killing you while you were still in the mountains and disposing of your body. It would have been neater that way than if he was supposedly found dead in one place and you in another."

"Then why didn't he kill me?"

"I don't know—yet. Maybe something came up that made him think it was safer to take eight hundred thousand than to take a greater risk for the one million three hundred thousand."

"It seems to me there is one flaw in your thinking, Mr. March," she said carefully. "If Richard planned and did what you suspect, how would he get the money? In the present case, your company will have to pay the money to me. As I've pointed out, Richard and I were not on the best of terms, so he couldn't plan arson and murder, and then think that I'd just turn all the money over to him."

"You might," I said. "He could always claim that you and he had planned the crime together, and you'd have trouble proving that it wasn't true. In a case like that, you might turn the money over to him, as long as there was enough left for you, rather than run the risk of being tried for arson and murder."

"And what if he killed me? The money would then have gone to a foundation. How would he have gotten it?"

"I don't know yet, but it's always possible that he set up the foundation himself with just this in mind, and had a plan that would enable him to get the money later."

"I see," she said. She got up and came over to where I sat. She took my glass and went over to the bar. She filled it and brought it back to me. "You mentioned two situations in which there might have been a point to killing the woman."

"So I did," I agreed. "It's always possible that you weren't as calm about your husband's girlfriends as you say. You might have seen the chance to get rid of him and his current woman and make a handsome profit at the same time."

She laughed. "After all, I was up in the mountains when all this happened."

"And the fire was set by professional arsonists. They could have been hired by you before you went off to establish your alibi."

"And I suppose you want to check what you call my alibi?"

"I'd like to talk to the woman who was with you. I could get her name and address from the police, but I thought I could get it from you just as easily."

"Of course," she said. "Her name is Debby Vance. She lives in the Montecito in Hollywood."

Her name sounded familiar. Then I remembered why. "The actress?" I asked.

"Yes. Debby's been my friend for ten years. In the last five years she's become quite successful. It couldn't have happened to a nicer person."

"You don't mind if I talk to her?"

"Would it make any difference if I did?"

"No."

"Then I don't mind," she said with a smile. "I don't suppose you'll believe her anyway. After all, she is my friend."

"I'll talk to others," I said. "What about your husband's business, Mrs. Cantwell? What kind of shape was it in?"

"I have no idea. Richard didn't approve of his wife knowing about business. But I presume it was doing very well. Richard never seemed to lack for money."

"That doesn't always mean that the business is doing well," I observed. "Tell me one more thing, Mrs. Cantwell, and then I won't bother you anymore today. If both of you had died, the insurance money would have gone to a foundation. What about the rest of the estate?"

"I haven't seen Richard's will yet," she said, "but he did tell me once that if we both died, everything would go to the foundation."

"Why?"

"I don't understand."

"Why the foundation? If he was the sort of man you say he was, he doesn't sound like a man who would leave his money to a cultural foundation."

"It's a little more complicated than that," she said. "First, we had no children and neither of us had any near relatives. Richard was disgusted with all political groups, and he didn't approve of charity. Since the last war Richard made most of his money on imports from Japan. He admired the Japanese—as businessmen, that is. So he started financing the foundation, not for cultural reasons but as something that he said was good business. I think it proved to be that for him, and therefore he changed his will and the insurance papers so that the foundation would get everything in the event both of us died."

"Do you know anything about the foundation?"

"No. Just its name—the Japanese-American Cultural Corporation—and that it's run by some Japanese woman. I don't recall her name."

"Since both of you didn't die," I said, "it changes the whole picture. If something happens to you before the estate is settled, I guess the foundation would still collect. But once everything is transferred to your name, you can change the picture. Will you?"

"I haven't thought about it," she said, "but I probably will. I haven't any burning desire to help Japanese-American business. Maybe I'll set up my own foundation one for unhappy wives."

"Complete with geisha boys?" I asked with a smile. "Well,

Mrs. Cantwell, I won't bother you anymore now. Thanks for being so patient with me."

"Don't run away," she said. "If you're through with the inquisition, why not stick around for a few drinks and just get acquainted?"

"It's tempting," I admitted, "but I'd better take a rain check on it. That'll give me an excuse to come back and see you another time."

"Promise?" she asked.

"Promise," I said. "I'll be back. For a drink."

"I'm glad you added that." She smiled. "I was afraid that you might only come back because you suspected me."

"I might for that reason, too," I said. "Good-bye, Mrs. Cantwell."

"Good-bye, Mr. March. I'll ring for Elizabeth to show you out."

"Don't bother. I can find my way." I took a last look at the salient points of the red dress and left the room. I went down the long stairway and out of the house. I felt as if I'd escaped from a trap, but the escape left me feeling sad.

I had intended to go directly to see the woman who had been with Pamela Cantwell, but then I had an impulse. I hadn't gotten too much from Mrs. Cantwell, and that always made me restless. I stopped off at a drugstore and called a man I knew on a Los Angeles newspaper. We cut up old touches for a few minutes and then I asked him if he knew where Harry Manfred was staying in town. He did. It was one of the better hotels in Beverly Hills. He wanted to know what was up and I promised him the story when there was one. I got back in my car and drove to the hotel.

It took a little time, but the desk clerk finally gave me Manfred's suite number and promised that he wouldn't call to say I was on my way up. I went to the tenth floor and knocked on the door. It was opened by a man wearing a three hundred dollar suit and about five cents' worth of friendliness.

"You've got the wrong door, chum," he said before I could say anything. "We ain't expecting anybody."

He started to close the door, but I put my foot in it. "You're only half right," I said. "You're not expecting anybody, but I don't have the wrong door. I want to see Manfred."

He looked interested in an unpleasant way. "Yeah? What's the pitch?"

"No pitch. I'm more of the catcher type. Who are you—the butler?"

He wasn't amused. "Who the hell are you?" he asked.

"Milo March. I want to see Harry Manfred."

His gaze didn't leave my face, but he raised his voice. "You know a Milo March, boss?"

"What's his racket?" a voice asked. It came from somewhere inside the suite.

"You heard him," the man in the doorway said.

"I'm in insurance," I said.

"Tell him I don't want any," the voice said.

The man in the doorway looked at me the way an exterminator might look at a room he was about to spray. "That's the way it is, chum. Take your foot out of the door before you lose it"

"That's not the way I heard it" I said. "I understand that you are interested in certain kinds of insurance."

"What the hell's going on?" the voice asked irritably. "Is it something you can't handle, Eddie?"

"I can handle it," Eddie said. He was looking at me more closely. "What kind of insurance, chum?"

"Fire," I said. "You know—gasoline and matches, or maybe a candle. Materials worth a dollar and a three hundred thousand dollar sale—plus a five hundred thousand dollar bonus. Even split two ways, it's a better contract than Jimmy Hoffa* could get."

For the first time since he'd opened the door, Eddie moved. There was a gun pointing at the spot where my belt buckled.

"Inside," he said. "And make it like you was walking on eggs, chum."

---

* Jimmy Hoffa, president of the teamsters' union at the time of this book's publication in 1963, was working toward a national contract for over-the-road truck drivers (it was achieved in 1964). His connections with organized crime were also well known. Hoffa disappeared in 1975 and the case has never been solved. (All footnotes were added by the editor.)

THREE

The room I entered was a small sitting room. There was nobody else in it. Just Eddie and me. There was a half-open door leading into another room, but I couldn't see into it. Eddie pressed the gun against me and used his free hand to search me. I hadn't brought my gun.

"What the hell's going on?" the voice from the other room demanded once more.

"This guy said he thought we ought to be interested in fire insurance," Eddie said. "So I thought you'd better see him. He's clean."

"Bring him in," the voice said.

"Okay, sucker," Eddie said. "In there."

I walked into the next room. There were two men in the room. One of them looked like Eddie's twin, even though his hair was dark instead of light. There was no question that the other one was Harry Manfred. He was a short, thick-shouldered, dark man wearing a purple silk dressing gown. He was sitting on the bed, leaning back against pillows. A pretty blond girl was working on his nails.

"Okay, honey," he said, taking his hand away from her. He looked at the man sitting in the chair. "Give her a fifty, Jim."

The man dug into his pocket and brought out a roll. He took a fifty-dollar bill from it and handed the bill to the girl.

"Oh, thank you, Mr. Manfred," the blonde said.

"Beat it, honey," he said pleasantly. "This is business." He waited until she was out of the room, then looked at me. "Jim always carries my money. It spoils the lines of my suit."

"That must be a serious problem," I said soberly. "I never thought about it before."

He suddenly remembered why I was there and frowned. "Now, what the hell is this all about?"

"The guy started talking about fire insurance," Eddie explained again.

"Why the hell should I want fire insurance?" Manfred asked.

"You ought to know it's a good investment," I said. "But I didn't say that I wanted to sell you any. In fact, I doubt that the company would sell you any."

"Then what the hell do you want?" he demanded. He scowled at me. "You an insurance dick?"

"Right on the first guess. Intercontinental Insurance."

"What's it got to do with me? I got no fire insurance."

"I know. But I think some of your clients have carried insurance with us."

"What's your name?"

"Milo March."

"March, March," he said. His face worked with concentration. "I know that name from somewhere. An insurance dick, huh?"

"That's right," I answered cheerfully.

His face was still contorted. Then, suddenly, he snapped his fingers. "I got it," he said. His gaze focused on me. "New

Orleans. The Painter. You're the guy who got him."*

"The Painter," I said. "Raoul Rouen. The last of a fine old family and one of the first among what some people call the Syndicate. But I didn't get him. I got some of his people. I put him out of business. But he got himself."

Harry Manfred was changing as I talked. In the beginning he'd been a big man bothered by a mosquito and not paying too much attention; now he was really seeing me for the first time. His face had hardened and his eyes had about as much expression as a pair of buttons. His two men were also giving me their full attention.

"You out to get me?" Manfred asked bluntly.

"Whatever gave you such an idea? Why should I be out to get you?"

"A lot of cops have tried it," he replied savagely. "Federal cops, state cops, city cops, hick cops. And nobody's pinned anything on me in the last ten years. Harry Manfred's as clean as they come."

"Maybe we ought to change laundries," I said.

"Boss ... ," Eddie said.

"Shut up," Manfred said without taking his gaze from me. "What the hell do you want, March?"

"I'm a fire buff. There was a good one out here in Santa Monica a few days ago. I couldn't get here in time. I thought maybe you might have seen it."

"I read about it," he said, "but that's all. Why ask me about it?"

"I'm curious about something," I said. "Are you working

---

* See *A Hearse of Another Color* by M.E. Chaber.

for half of a million three hundred thousand dollars or only half of eight hundred thousand?"

"I ain't working." Manfred snapped his fingers and the man he'd called Jim gave him a cigarette and lit it. "I'm on a vacation."

"From what?"

"My business interests." He was getting more relaxed. "All of them legal."

"All?"

"All," he said emphatically. He sat up on the bed and shoved a pudgy finger in my direction. "You ask the FBI. They'll tell you that they can't prove anything else. That kid, Kennedy,* said that he would get me. Me—Harry Manfred. But nobody's got anything on me and nobody's going to get anything. I'm clean."

"Maybe," I said easily. "You're a big man now, Harry. Bigger than you were in the days when they used to drag you in for pimping or manslaughter. And more careful. Maybe you have money enough and are careful enough so that nothing can be pinned on you, but what about your boys?"

"What about them?"

"Maybe I'll get them. They're not as big and not as careful as you are. Maybe it'll be Eddie here—or Jim. Or some of the others. They must be around. It's a closing circle, Harry. And it always closes on somebody. Today it may be Eddie—tomorrow it may be you."

"Get out," he said.

"I'll get out," I said cheerfully, "but I won't go far. Remember the Painter."

* Robert F. Kennedy, U.S. Attorney General at the time.

"I'll remember the Painter," he said hoarsely. "He was a right guy. Maybe you better take out a little insurance yourself, March."

"Not me. It offers too much temptation. I'll see you around, Harry."

"Yeah," he said. "I'll keep you in mind, March."

"You do that," I told him. "Keep the home fires burning." I turned and left the room without looking back.

I drove down to Hollywood to the Montecito. I parked in the back and went in to the desk. Debby Vance was in and said she'd see me. I went up to the fourth floor and knocked on her door. She opened it and invited me in. She was a little thing with reddish-blond hair, a pixie face, and a body with more curves than a mountain trail.

"I guess Mrs. Cantwell called you," I said when I was in the apartment.

"Why do you say that?" she countered.

"It figures. I told her I wanted to talk to you and she gave me your address. So it's natural that she would call and warn you that I was coming around to check on her alibi. Otherwise you wouldn't have invited me up so quickly."

She laughed. "Pam was right. She said that you were a shrewd one and that I shouldn't try to play any games. Will you have some coffee with me, Mr. March?"

"Sure."

"Reinforced? I have some very good brandy."

"Reinforced by all means. I like to guard against colds."

She laughed again and went into the kitchen. She was soon back with two cups of coffee and two jiggers of brandy. I took mine and poured the brandy in the coffee. I tasted it. It was good coffee and good brandy.

"I've seen you in several of your pictures," I said, "and admired you."

"Pam said you'd probably flatter me, too, but I love it. She also said that you're suspicious of her. Why?"

"I'm paid to be suspicious. Why did you and Mrs. Cantwell go to the mountains?"

"We usually go every year for a week or so. Pam and I are very old friends, but we don't see each other too often, except when we take a vacation like that. And for me, especially, it's wonderful. There's no phone, no radio, no television, nothing but just quiet rest. My agent always screams that I'm losing a fortune when I go, but I love every minute of it."

"How long were you up there this time?" I asked.

"Six days."

"Coming back when?"

"Yesterday."

"And that was the first time you knew anything about the fire and the two deaths?"

"Yes. There isn't even any mail up there."

"It must have been quite a shock to Mrs. Cantwell," I observed.

"The same sort of shock it was to me. Such things are always shocking."

"But more so when it's your husband or your wife."

"You're fishing, Mr. March," she said, waving a finger at me. "It was no secret that Pam had a marriage of convenience and that was all. Richard Cantwell was a bum, and that was no secret either. It's too bad that he had to die that way—but he's still no loss."

"What did you and Mrs. Cantwell do while you were up there?"

"Slept and read, played Scrabble and chess, and went skiing three or four times. That's all."

"Did you have any visitors while you were there?"

"No."

"See anybody else at all?"

"No."

"Was Mrs. Cantwell nervous or upset during those days?"

"Of course not. And neither one of us needed any sleeping pills to get to sleep at night."

"You came back on the day you had planned to?"

"Yes."

"Mrs. Cantwell was with you all the time?"

"Yes. Except when we were asleep and even then she was in the next room."

"Could she have come back to the city and then returned without you knowing it?"

"Absolutely not."

"All right," I said. "Did anything happen while you were up in the mountains?"

"What do you mean?" she asked.

"What happened? What did you do? How did the days and the evenings pass? Did anything unusual happen at all?"

"I told you," she said. "We slept a lot. We both like to read, and we had several new books with us. We played Scrabble and had a few chess games. We went skiing the first three or four days, but then we didn't go anymore after our narrow escape."

"What narrow escape?"

"It was either the third or fourth day. We were skiing in our usual spot when there was a snowslide up on the mountain above us. About two million tons of snow came sliding down that mountain and almost caught us. So we hung up the skis and left them there."

"What caused the snowslide?"

"I don't know. Maybe the sun melted it just enough."

"Or maybe somebody started it."

She looked startled. "What do you mean?"

"Mrs. Cantwell told you that I was suspicious of her, but I guess she didn't tell you that I had a few other ideas in mind, too."

"I don't get it," she said. "Who would do anything like that?"

"How about Richard Cantwell as a starter?"

"But he's dead." Suddenly her eyes widened and she looked at me. "Isn't he?"

"Maybe," I said. "I don't know. I have an open mind about it. There are a couple of possibilities. Maybe Richard Cantwell made a deal with his wife. He apparently dies and she collects his insurance and the fire insurance, and then when everything has calmed down they meet somewhere else. In the meantime, he sets off an avalanche of snow where she's busy establishing an alibi so that it will look as if someone tried to kill her, too. Or maybe Richard Cantwell staged his own apparent death and planned on actually killing his wife so that a foundation, which he in some way controls, collects on everything."

"I might buy the second possibility," she said. "Richard Cantwell was a no-good bastard who might have done anything. But the police say that his body was identified."

"There wasn't much to identify. Mostly teeth. You can buy teeth."

"You mean that you think Richard Cantwell is still alive?"

"I don't know," I admitted, "but I intend to find out. As I said, there are several possibilities."

"I don't believe that other one," she said flatly. "Pamela and I have been friends for years and I know her as well as I know myself. She wouldn't have helped her husband with any of his schemes, and certainly not one like that. The only reason she didn't leave him was because he wouldn't let her. Oh, she had all the charge accounts she could want, but he never let her have any money."

"She'll have plenty now," I observed.

"I'm glad," she said. She smiled at me. "Would you like some more coffee? Reinforced?"

"Not now," I said. "I'll take a rain check, if you don't mind."

"Anytime," she said. "I like handsome men—even when they are suspicious of my best friends."

"I'll remember," I told her. I left her apartment, escorted by her perfume, which kept pulling me back. It was one of the many times I've regretted working for a living.

The Cantwell Import Company was on Fifth Street in downtown Los Angeles. It was a street of warehouses and offices, a block away from the busy main street and a block away from the equally busy Skid Row. I parked the Cadillac on the street and walked into the Cantwell offices. I told the receptionist what I wanted, and I was shortly shown into an office. It was occupied by a small man with a receding hairline and a thin mustache. He sat behind a large desk as though he didn't feel he belonged there.

"This is Mr. Patman," the receptionist said to me. She turned and left.

"You're the business manager, Mr. Patman?" I asked.

"I believe so," he said. He smiled nervously. "I'm really not sure. You see, Mr. Cantwell was the only manager this business ever had. He wouldn't allow anyone to do anything that was important. That is, when he was alive. Now, I don't know. I was glad to hear that Mrs. Cantwell is alive. She said for me to take charge."

"What did you do in the company before, Mr. Patman?"

"I was the accountant. Of course, Mr. Cantwell worked very closely with me, so you might say I knew quite a bit about the business. Yes, I think you could say that."

"How long did you work for Cantwell?" I asked.

"Twenty-five years next month."

"Then you must have known Cantwell and his company very well."

"Yes. Yes, I believe you could say that."

"And did you know Mrs. Cantwell?"

"Yes, of course, but not so well. She seldom came down here and I was never invited to the house—except when I might have to take some papers to Mr. Cantwell there."

"You know why I'm here?" I asked.

"The girl said you were from the insurance company, so I presume you are here in connection with the two policies concerned. Isn't that so?"

I nodded. "You are familiar with Cantwell's insurance policies?"

"Oh, yes, I know all the policies very well. I might say that I gave a certain amount of advice on them. When I was asked, of course."

"Good," I said. "You're just the man I want to talk to. What did you think of Mr. Cantwell?"

He looked startled. "Well, he—he was a very astute businessman. He started this business and built it up."

"I'm sure he did," I said pleasantly. "But what did you think of him personally? Did you enjoy working for him? Did others? What kind of a boss was he?"

"Personally," he repeated, as though he wasn't sure what the word meant. He took a pair of glasses from his pocket and began cleaning them. "I'm not sure that I ever thought of Mr. Cantwell in the personal sense."

"You must have. Did anyone in the office like him?"

"I do not believe in speaking ill of the dead," he said primly.

"Nonsense, man," I said roughly. "We're not just talking about a man who is merely dead. We're talking about Richard Cantwell, a man who couldn't get along with anybody, including his wife, a man who collected mistresses the way some men collect stamps, and a man who was either murdered or murdered someone else in an attempt to defraud the insurance company."

Patman put on the glasses, stared through them for a

minute, then put them back in his pocket. His face worked nervously. "Well," he said finally, "Mr. Cantwell was sometimes rather difficult."

"I'll bet. How did the other employees feel about him?"

"I'm afraid Mr. Cantwell was not popular with them—except for an occasional temporary popularity with one person."

"You mean a girl with whom he would be having an affair?"

"Yes."

"Any of them working here now?"

"No. It was customary to discharge them—afterwards."

"A nice fellow," I said. "How did he treat you?"

"He paid me well, although good salaries were not a habit with him."

"I didn't ask you that. I asked how he treated you."

"Like a servant." He bit the words off as if each one were a slice of lemon peel.

"You were with him twenty-five years. Anyone else here who was with him that long?"

"No. When the company was first started there were only three of us: Mr.

Cantwell, Hal Kray, and myself. It was Kray who had certain contacts which brought in the first business we got. He was given some small percentage of the company, so you might say that I was the only employee."

"Is this Kray still a partner?"

"No. About five years ago the business was reorganized and he no longer retained an interest. A few weeks later he was fired. I do not know what reason was given."

"Where is he now?"

"I do not know. I haven't seen him since then."

"Any other employees been here long?"

"The longest is a little less than two years. As I said, Mr. Cantwell did not pay good salaries and we have a rapid turnover."

"All right," I said, "let's go on to something else. Do you know anything about this foundation that is the second beneficiary in the insurance policies?"

"The Japanese-American Cultural Corporation? Of course I do. I helped to set it up."

"Tell me about it," I said.

He put the tips of his fingers together and stared off over my head. "The Japanese-American Cultural Corporation was founded about three years ago. It is a nonprofit corporation. Its purpose is to improve the relations between this country and Japan."

"What does it do?" I interrupted.

"Arranges for cultural exchanges," he said. "It sponsors, and sometimes pays part of the cost for, the translations from one language to the other. It arranges for the exhibition and sale of American art objects in Japan and for Japanese art here. It has been instrumental in the exchange of theater and sports groups. It publishes pamphlets in English on Japan and in Japanese on America. It does almost everything possible to help the two countries understand each other."

"Very commendable. But why? What was Cantwell's relationship to this?"

"He was the original donor and has in the past three years

given about three-fourths of the money spent by the foundation."

"Why? He doesn't strike me as having been the sort of man who was interested in doing anything for art. Was the broad one of his mistresses?"

"The broad? Oh, I presume you mean Miss Asakura." He looked thoughtful for a minute. "She's a very attractive young lady, so I suppose it's possible, but I never had any clear indication that she was."

"Then why?"

"I've thought about that myself," he confessed. "I think, perhaps, there were several reasons. Miss Asakura is related to the owner of a company in Japan with which we do considerable business. That business did increase shortly thereafter. I believe that Mr. Cantwell's participation in the foundation—which was well publicized in Japan—brought in much more business. I'm sure that Mr. Cantwell anticipated these things. And they were probably his chief reasons for supporting the foundation. Making the foundation the second beneficiary in the insurance policies was probably something else. Mr. Cantwell had no family and no friends. He had no old employees except me. I believe it amused him to think that if anything happened to him, all the money would go to another country, one with which we had been at war not too long ago. That is, the money would go to benefit it."

"Is the business successful?" I asked.

"Yes, indeed. It has become more successful with each year."

"So it's in good shape?"

"What do you mean?"

"Has someone been dipping into the till?" I asked bluntly. "If so, then it may not be in such good shape no matter how successful it's been."

He had turned pale while I was talking. He took the glasses from his pocket again, looked at them, then replaced them. His hands were trembling. "Whatever gave you that idea?" he asked.

"The insurance company received an anonymous letter not long ago suggesting that such was the case. I probably would have gotten around to asking the same question even if they hadn't."

He took a deep breath. "I wouldn't want any rumors like that to get out just now, Mr. March. It might hurt the business for Mrs. Cantwell. I am not sure, you understand, but I believe that there may have been certain defalcations."

"How much?"

"I'm not sure," he faltered. "I just today discovered something that makes me think this is true. But I have had no opportunity to look into it further, and it may very well take several days to trace."

"Make a guess," I said.

He wasn't happy about it, but he'd gone too far to back down. "I would guess that it was somewhere in the neighborhood of five hundred thousand dollars."

"That's a lovely neighborhood," I said. "Who could have done it?"

"Only one person could have taken a dollar from this company," he said. "That was Mr. Cantwell. No one else had access to any of the funds."

"How could he have done it without you knowing it? You were the accountant."

"I operated entirely on memoranda given to me by Mr. Cantwell. That was the way we always worked."

"All right," I said. "Any idea why he might do it? Was he heavily in debt?"

"I wouldn't think so. Mr. Cantwell did spend a lot of money, but then he also had a good income. Even if that were so, Mr. March, it doesn't make any sense. This was Mr. Cantwell's company. He *was* the company. He didn't have to steal the money and have the books falsified. He could have just drawn the money out in a normal manner. He didn't have to account to anyone."

"But somebody would have had to know he was taking the money if he did it that way. At least you would have known. Maybe he wanted to get the money without anyone knowing he had it."

He looked bewildered. "But why?"

"I can think of a few reasons," I said. "Tell me something else, Mr. Patman. Did you know much about his mistresses?"

He shook his head. "I knew he had them, that was about all. Sometimes it would be a girl here and we'd all know about it. But that wasn't often. Other times I could guess he was starting up with a new one. Whenever that happened, he'd be absent from the office more for the first couple of weeks. But I never knew any of them."

"Any idea of who his latest mistress was?"

"No."

"There was a woman's body found with the one identified

as Cantwell's," I said. "Who do you think that might have been?"

"I don't know."

I wasn't getting anywhere with that, so I switched back to the money. "When would you say that he began to help himself to the company funds?"

"I can't say for sure until I've had a chance to go over his papers and checkbook more carefully, but I believe it might have been during the last three months."

"What about Cantwell's behavior during that period? Would you say that it was normal?"

He was thoughtful for a minute. "Pretty much so, I believe."

"Did he acquire a new mistress during that period?"

"I think so," he said uncertainly. "I can't really be sure. I never paid close attention to the exact times. Not after all these years."

"Did he do anything unusual during this time?"

"No. Nothing important."

"What do you mean by that? If he did anything unusual tell me about it, even if you think it unimportant."

"Well," he said, "when Mr. Cantwell was at the office he always went to a hotel over near Pershing Square for his lunch. But there were several days about two months ago when I saw him going into bars near here. You know the sort of places I mean, certainly not the sort of bars that a man like Mr. Cantwell would normally enter."

"You mean Skid Row bars?"

"Yes."

"Was it always the same bar?"

"No, each time a different one. Although I believe that the last time I saw him, he was entering one that I'd seen him go into before."

"Remember what bar it was?"

"I'm sorry, I don't"

"When he returned on those days, was there any evidence that he'd been drinking heavily?"

"No."

"Did he drink much?"

"Not to excess, so far as I know. I believe he usually had one or two drinks before lunch and perhaps a few drinks at night, but so far as I know that was all."

"Any idea why he went to those bars?"

He shook his head.

"That period was the only time you ever saw him do such a thing?"

"Yes."

"All right, Mr. Patman," I said, standing up. "I won't take up any more of your time now. I'll check back with you in a few days about the auditing of the books."

"Mr. March," he said nervously, "I do hope that you won't say anything about the—er—shortage?"

"Only to my insurance company," I said. I started to leave, then turned back. "Tell me one more thing, Mr. Patman. Considering the sort of man Cantwell was and the way he treated you, why did you stay with him so long?"

"I believe I said that he did pay me well." He looked up at me and there was a sort of nakedness in his eyes. "I guess I stayed for another reason. I thought that someday he would get what was coming to him and I wanted to be around to see it happen." He took the glasses from his pocket and was busy cleaning them again as I left.

FOUR

There was a street not far from the import offices that was filled with cheap bars. Human derelicts, in various stages of stupor, wandered in and out of them or collapsed on the sidewalk. The street was full of the smell of stale whiskey and wine and stale clothing. A police wagon pulled up and a half dozen comatose men were loaded into it as I turned the corner.

I had to start somewhere. The first bar I came to was called the Shamrock. I turned and went inside. It was like a million bars all over the country. It smelled of beer and whiskey and smoke. Down at one end of the bar there were four men. All of them needed shaves and baths and fresh clothes and none of them needed, from the looks of them, the glasses of wine over which they nodded. The bartender didn't look much better, but at least he was sober. Sober and bored. He looked up from a racing form and showed some surprise at the sight of me. He put down the form and came over.

I looked around at the bar. The mirror back of it was plastered with prices. Almost any shot of American whiskey was thirty or thirty-five cents. A few brands were forty cents. And you could get any imported whiskey for a mere fifty cents. I settled for V.O. and water. The bartender poured the drink into a shot glass that seemed to be made out of magnifying glass. It was probably slightly less than an ounce. He waited carefully for the money, rang it up, and went back to his racing form.

I sipped my drink and looked around. The four men at the end of the bar wouldn't do me much good. They were about ready for the sidewalk and the police wagon.

I felt rather than heard someone else come in. I looked around. It was another bum. But this one seemed reasonably sober. Also a little cleaner. He needed a shave and his clothes were pretty battered, but he didn't look as if he'd just rolled in the gutter. He paid no attention to me or the other four men as he walked up to the bar.

"Good afternoon, William," he said. The tones were those of an educated man.

The bartender looked up and frowned. "Hello, Hank," he said. "What do you want?"

The newcomer considered the question as carefully as if it involved the fate of the world. "I believe," he said finally, "I will have a glass of 'the grape that can with logic absolute the two-and-seventy jarring sects confute.'"

"Words," the bartender said scornfully. "All you ever have, Hank, is words. You got the two bits for the glass of wine?"

The man made a pretense of feeling through his pockets. "I believe," he said, "that I am temporarily without funds, but if you could 'fetch me somewhat to delight my mind,' I might be able to manage a restitution on the morrow."

"Words," the bartender said again. "No money, no booze. Is that clear?"

"Painfully so," the man said.

"Just a minute," I said. "I'll buy him a drink, bartender. Give him anything he wants."

The man turned and looked at me. His eyes were still bright and clear, not yet clouded by cheap liquor. His gaze was inquisitive. "By my faith," he said, "a good Samaritan. I thought they had gone out of fashion. Did you say anything, sir?"

"I did," I told him.

"Then, innkeeper, I will have whiskey. The best you have in the house."

"Give him the same as I have," I said, "some V.O." The bartender looked his disapproval, but he took the bottle and poured a drink. He came down and took the money from me.

"Why don't you come down and join me," I said to the man.

"Delighted," he said. He carried his drink down to sit next to me. He took a sip from the glass. "An excellent whiskey, sir," he said. "I had almost forgotten there were such delights in the world."

"Enjoy it," I said. "Any man who can quote from both Khayyam and Marlowe almost in the same breath deserves it."

"Ah," he said, "you recognized both quotations?" He gave me a searching look. "I do not recall seeing you before, sir. You do not have the appearance of a regular denizen of this fleshpot. Nor do we often have visitors who recognize Omar or Christopher—if I may be familiar."

"I don't imagine that either of them would object to being discussed in a tavern." I said. "My name is Milo March. I'm just passing through."

"An excellent thing to be doing anywhere in the world," he said. He lifted his glass. "Your most excellent health, sir." He finished the drink.

I finished my own and motioned for the bartender to fill both glasses. He did, but his expression indicated that he didn't think it was a good idea. I paid him and let him drift back to his racing form.

"I'm not sure that I caught your name," I said to the man.

He smiled without mirth. "Perhaps because I did not mention it, sir. Here I am known simply as Hank. It is not an area which specializes in elaborate identification."

"All right, Hank," I said. I lifted my glass. "To your good fortune."

We both drank. There was a vague muttering from the four drunks at the end of the bar. Hank looked at them.

" 'These lords, perhaps,' " he said, " 'do scorn our estimates, and think we prattle with distempered spirits.' "

"I always say that distempered spirits are the best kind," I said gravely. "And I think Marlowe might have agreed. Tell me, Hank, what is this preoccupation with our friend of bygone years, Christopher Marlowe?"

"A fine writer," he said. "In fact, sir, I believe he was the finest writer in the English language, perhaps in any language."

"There was a fellow named Shakespeare," I said casually.

He looked at me with interest. "A man of obvious financial worth who knows Marlowe and Shakespeare, and also frequents low taverns. You try my credulity, sir. I would think that you would be more at home in the Brown Derby with a martini in your hand."

"I like those, too, but I don't like to get in a rut. You were saying something about the finest writer in the English language ..."

"Christopher Marlowe," he said firmly. "I grant that he did not reach the peak achieved by Shakespeare, but then Marlowe was murdered when he was only twenty-nine years of age. Nearly everything he wrote was written when he was considerably younger than that. If you compare his first works with those of Shakespeare, and also compare the improvement in each writer over a similar period of time, I think you might agree with me. I might mention that I think Shakespeare knew this; Marlowe was the only contemporary that Shakespeare mentioned in his plays."

" 'A great reckoning in a little room,' " I murmured.

"You astound me, sir," he said. "What manner of man are you, who wears, if I may venture a guess, a Brooks Brothers suit, drinks in a Skid Row bar, and quotes Shakespeare on Marlowe?"

"With the possible exception of the suit," I said, "I could ask you the same question." Our glasses were empty and I motioned to the bartender to fill them up again. "But it's not so mysterious, Hank. I am a man who enjoys reading, wenching, and drinking—not necessarily in that order. I can get the same vintage of V.O. in this bar as I could in a fancy one, and this one happened to be the nearest. As for the clothes, I like good clothes and I can usually afford them, thanks to an active interest in the more violent aspects of our civilization."

"Violence? Do you mean murder?"

"Sometimes murder."

"How interesting. Are you some species of well-dressed fuzz?"

"I don't think the cops would like it if you called me a cop," I said. "Just say that I'm interested in such things, and that sometimes I make money from my interest."

"Most people are interested in murder," he said. "That is, when Death also comes softly in the night 'on little cat feet.' "

"Sometimes it walks heavier than that," I said. "Do you come in here regularly, Hank?"

"You might say that I am a loyal patron of this and every other tavern on the street, subject only to the state of my finances. It is my contribution to the better things in life. 'I often wonder what the vintners buy one half so precious as the goods they sell.' "

"I'll go along with that," I said. "I gather from what you said that it isn't too often that you see a well-dressed man in these bars."

"Affluence is not one of the more prominent aspects of the section," he said. "We are mostly bound together by the sameness of our existence. And you, sir?"

"About two months ago there was a man who visited the bars along here for several days. He was a very prosperous businessman with offices not far from here. He was a big spender and was, I'm sure, dressed in a very expensive suit. He must have been conspicuous."

"I remember there was such a man around. Why are you interested?"

"I want to know why he was visiting these bars."

"Perhaps he was merely rehearsing for a future existence.

Perhaps he had decided to give up a life of responsibility and join us in the ultimate freedom."

"Perhaps—but I doubt it. Did you see him often?"

"Five or six times, maybe more. I tried to be present at all times. There was a generous flow of refreshments when he was here."

"Why?" I asked. "You're a man of some curiosity. You've just shown it with me, so you must have been curious about him. Why did he come to one of these bars every day for about a week and then suddenly stop coming?"

"I confess to a curiosity about the activities of my fellow humans," he said. "I was, in fact, interested in the man's behavior. But I'm afraid I was never able to determine his purpose—except that he was looking for someone."

"Who?"

He was thoughtful for a minute, staring at the empty glass in his hand. I took the hint and ordered another round from the bartender.

"You are a gentleman and a scholar," Hank said. "I don't believe that 'who' is proper terminology. Perhaps, in the beginning at least, he was looking for a *what,* rather than a *who.*"

"What does that mean?"

"I believe that he was looking for a type of man, a certain appearance and build. One who was not too far gone, but was well on his way."

"Why here?"

"I gave that some thought at the time, sir. My first idea was that the man was some variety of sexual deviate, but I soon discarded that. Later I thought he was merely rich and eccentric, a man without kith or kin, looking for someone to salvage from our particular version of the city dump, someone he could rebuild in his own image, you might say."

"Why do you put it that way?" I asked.

"Most of the men in whom he seemed interested were about his own size and build and age, with perhaps other superficial resemblances. And there are rich men who like to play god."

"Not only rich men," I said. "Did he finally find someone?"

"I believe so."

"You don't know?"

"Only in a deductive sense. The last two days, he spent all his time with one man, but even Jimmy didn't know what he wanted. He said that the man just kept buying him drinks and asking a lot of questions about himself."

"Who was it he picked?"

"Jimmy."

"Last name?"

He shrugged. "We're not much for last names around here. I don't know what it was and I don't think anyone else does." He raised his voice. "William."

"Yeah?" the bartender said.

"What was Jimmy's last name?"

"How the hell do I know?" the bartender said. "Half the time around this joint I don't even know my own last name." He went back to his racing form.

"You see," Hank said. "We do not consider labels so important. He was Jimmy, and that was all anyone needed to know."

"All right," I said. "Any idea where I can find Jimmy?"

"I fear not. He has not been around here since then. Oh, he was here for one extra day after the last time the other man was seen. He visited every bar, seemed to be in an unusually solvent state, and bought drinks for everyone. The following day he was gone. It is also part of my deduction that he was, shall we say, adopted by the man who found him. On the other hand, perhaps Jimmy was his long-lost brother."

"What about Jimmy's friends? They might be able to tell me where to find him."

"Alas, here one has no friends, except when one has a bottle to share. It is actually a most convenient arrangement. When Jimmy came into good fortune, he did in a way share a bottle with everyone. But if my theory is correct, he was then coming into possession of a bottle much too large to share, and so he would vanish without even saying good-bye. I would do the same myself."

"Are you sure no one will know where he went? Perhaps at the place where he lived."

He smiled. "Like many of us, he did not have what you could call a permanent address. It depended on whether he had fifty cents for a bed, or twenty-five cents, or nothing. No mail is ever received at any of these addresses, so there is no reason for leaving a forwarding address. What is to be forwarded—an old Muscatel bottle?"

"I suppose you're right," I said. Actually, I wasn't too surprised by the information; it fit the picture I already had in mind. All that was required was to find all the pieces and put them together. "Do you think you could find out anything about what Jimmy did or where he went after meeting this other man?"

"I do not know," he said. "As I have told you, there is little available information about anyone on Skid Row."

"Will you try?"

"I shall endeavor to make inquiries."

"That's all I can ask," I said. "I'll come back down here and look for you. Or if you think there is something urgent, I can be reached at the Pacific-Melton Hotel in Santa Monica." I took a ten-dollar bill from my pocket and beckoned the bartender over. I put the bill on the bar. "I want you to take this," I told him, "and give Hank ten dollars' worth of credit. Be sure that he gets all of it."

The bartender scowled, but he put the money in the cash register and made a note on a slip of paper.

" 'O friend,' " Hank said, " 'I feel thy words to comfort my distressed soul.' "

"You left out part of the quotation," I said: " 'so I will leave you a while to ponder on your sins.' "

He smiled as I got up and walked out. I went around the corner and got into the Cadillac. I looked at my watch. Most of the day was gone, but I could still do a couple of things. I checked the notes I'd made. The Japanese-American Cultural Corporation had offices out in Hollywood. I drove across town and headed up Sunset Boulevard. On the way, I stopped at a drugstore and made a phone call to Pamela Cantwell. She answered it herself.

"This is Milo March," I said.

"Hello," she said. "Have you decided to have me arrested?"

"Not immediately," I said. "In fact, I had something quite different in mind."

"Oh?"

"Since you're not in heavy mourning," I said, "I thought you might have dinner with me tonight."

"Do you always socialize with the people you suspect of crimes?" she asked.

"Only sometimes," I said cheerfully. "I promise not to be too suspicious. How about it?"

She hesitated only a moment. "I'd love to."

"Fine. I'll pick you up about seven?"

"I'll be ready. Good-bye, Mr. March." There was a click as she hung up.

I went back to the car and drove to Hollywood. The foundation had its offices in a new modernistic building. I parked and went up. There was a pretty Japanese girl at the reception desk.

"My name is Milo March," I said. "I'd like to see Miss Asakura. Tell her it's in reference to the foundation and its original sponsor."

She smiled and picked up her phone. She talked for a minute, then replaced the receiver. She gave me another one of those smiles. "You may go in," she said, indicating a door on my left.

I walked over and opened the door. I took one step inside and then stopped. The girl was standing up back of her desk. She was no more than five feet tall and looked like a Japanese doll—only she had a lot more curves than most of the Japanese women I'd seen. I realized that I'd been staring a long time. I stepped farther into the room and closed the door behind me. "Miss Asakura?" I asked.

"Yes," she said. She smiled as though she knew what I'd been thinking while I was standing in the doorway. "What can I do for you, Mr. March?"

"That's a large question," I said. "It has to do directly with Richard Cantwell and indirectly with your foundation. I'd like to ask you a few questions."

"Certainly," she said. "Won't you sit down, please? I was very sorry to learn about the accident to Mr. Cantwell."

We both sat down. I discovered that she looked even better at close range than she had at a distance. "We're not sure it was an accident, Miss Asakura," I said. "I'll be perfectly frank with you; I represent the insurance company which carried all of Cantwell's insurance. As you may know, the life insurance on himself and on his wife, as well as the fire insurance on the house that burned down, carried a clause that in the event that he and his wife died simultaneously, all of the money was to go to your foundation."

She laughed softly. "I see. You think that perhaps someone here at the foundation might have had a hand in the fire and the death of Mr. Cantwell. But the papers today have reported that Mrs. Cantwell is still very much alive, so you see we do not get any money from the insurance policies of Mr. Cantwell. Far from having gained by this, we have actually lost, since Mr. Cantwell was a steady donor to our cause."

"That wasn't actually my theory," I said mildly, "and I'd still like to ask you a few questions."

"All right. I'll answer if I can."

"How long did you know Mr. Cantwell?"

"Oh, several years. Strangely enough, I first met him in Japan. I was visiting my uncle who owns the Asakura Corporation there. Mr. Cantwell did considerable business with my uncle's company."

"You became friends?"

"We became friendly, yes."

"How friendly?" I asked bluntly.

She laughed again. "You are frank, aren't you, Mr. March? I'll try to answer you just as frankly. I'm aware that Mr. Cantwell was very interested in women, many women. I will not deny that there were times when he tried to turn our relationship into something else, but it was never more than friendly."

"I can't blame him for trying," I said. "Whose idea was this foundation? His or yours?"

"Mine," she said promptly. "I'd had the idea for a long time. I mentioned it that time at my uncle's house in Japan. Mr. Cantwell was interested, and told me to come and see him when we both got back here. I did and that was the beginning of the foundation."

"He put up all the original money?"

"Yes."

"And most of it since then?"

"Yes."

"Has any of the money come from other sources?"

"Yes, but not nearly as much as Mr. Cantwell gave."

"How much would you say he has given the foundation from the beginning?"

"About two hundred thousand dollars."

"That's a lot of money," I said. "Why did he do it? Was he interested in Oriental culture or cementing friendship between Japan and this country?"

"Did you know Mr. Cantwell?" she countered.

"No, but I've been learning a lot about him."

"Then you should know that the answer to both questions is no. He was interested in making money, and I'm sure that he made a very good return on the money he put into the foundation. That was all right with me, because the foundation has still been accomplishing what I wanted it to do."

"What is that?"

"I am both American and Japanese," she said. "There is no way I can stop being Japanese, but I am also most thoroughly American. I want my fellow Americans to know more about the Japanese, and I want the Japanese to know more about me and my fellow Americans. If that can be accomplished, we might never have repetition of the things that happened here on the West Coast during World War II."

"I can't argue with that," I said. "But what now? As you pointed out, Mrs. Cantwell is still alive and you don't get any money. Cantwell isn't around to contribute more. Will you be able to continue?"

"I think so. We may have to trim expenses some, but I think we can continue. We do have a few other small donors now, and I'm sure they will continue. There are others I think we can get. And I thought I would go talk to Mrs. Cantwell after a suitable time."

"I doubt if that will do you much good," I said. "Who runs the foundation?"

"Well, I'm active head of it, if that's what you mean."

"Who signs the checks?"

"I do."

"Who makes the decisions?"

"We have a board of directors. They make all the decisions, based on recommendations from me, then I carry them out."

"Was Cantwell on the board?"

"No."

"What was his position in the corporation?"

"He didn't have any position in it."

"None. What about voting rights?"

"He had none."

"Then tell me something, Miss Asakura. If the foundation had come into a large amount of money, how could Cantwell have gotten his hands on it?"

"He couldn't have."

"Except through you?"

"Except through me." She smiled again. "Ah, I see were back to the mistress theory."

"The thought did occur to me," I admitted, "but I'll take your word for it. Well, I guess that's all for now. I may think of some other question to ask you later."

"Come back anytime, Mr. March," she said. "Maybe you'll become interested enough to give us a donation yourself."

"I'll come around sometime and let you give me a sales talk," I said.

I left and went downstairs. I found the nearest phone booth

and called the local office of Intercontinental. I asked them to have their lawyers check up on the Japanese-American Cultural Corporation. I wanted to know how it was set up and about everybody connected with it. They promised they'd have the information sometime the next day. I got back into my car and drove to Santa Monica. I'd have time for a couple of leisurely drinks and to change clothes before I went to pick up Pamela Cantwell.

I parked the car on the hotel grounds and went into the main building. There was a pleasant, dimly lit bar. It was almost empty. I sat at the bar and ordered a dry martini.

I sipped the drink and thought about the case. It was a tough one. I felt I had gotten off on the right track, although I'd have to dig up a lot to make a case out of it. But I had the beginning.

Richard Cantwell had taken something close to a half million dollars out of his company by dipping into the till. The only possible reason for doing it that way was that he didn't want anyone to know that he had the money in his pocket. He had also spent a week or so on Skid Row, searching for a bum who resembled him in general appearance and age. He'd found someone and that particular bum had also vanished. I'd still have to find an explanation for the dental identification, but that could have been fixed, so that the body in the fire might have been that of the man I knew only as Jimmy. A problem that still bothered me was that of the woman's body found in the fire. Who was she? And why was she there? I had one idea, but that might be the hardest of all to prove.

Maybe Pamela and Richard Cantwell had planned it

together. Maybe the two bodies were supposed to have been identified as Mr. and Mrs. Cantwell. Maybe she'd gone along that far, and then decided not to go the rest of the route. That would leave her sitting pretty, collecting all the insurance money, while her husband was left whistling out in limbo. That would be a pretty way of giving him the business if she hated him. But if that were true, Richard Cantwell was certainly not the type of man to take it sitting down, and sooner or later he'd show up with ideas of his own.

There was also the avalanche that had almost caught Pamela Cantwell and her friend on the mountain. That could have been a real avalanche or it could have been an attempt to kill her. The second possibility would fit in with my other theory. Suppose the whole thing was the scheme of Richard Cantwell. He goes out and finds himself a bum who more or less matches him physically and who won't be missed by anyone. He finds a way to make the teeth match and arranges to have the bum in the house when the torch is put to it. That might not be too hard, since he's also going to have a woman there. A woman who matches the description of his wife and will be identified as her. Then he has his wife killed else-where, in a place where she probably would never be found, and the stage is set. If he gets away with it, he stands to collect one million eight hundred thousand dollars, counting the half million taken from the business. Tax-free.

It was an idea that might attract a better man than Rich-ard Cantwell. It was also a good theory. But it did bring up a few questions for which I had no answers. The first one was, Why? He was making a lot of money and lived his life as he wanted to. Why change that? If he could steal a half million from himself, then he should have had enough money. And Patman had said the business was making more money every year. But there was another question. If that had been his plan, and if it had gone through, including the death of his wife, how had he planned to collect the money when one million three hundred thousand of it would have gone to the Japanese-American Cultural Corporation? At that point the only route I could see was through Kayoko Asakura—and that was the most scenic route I'd seen in a long time. Yet she had seemed completely sincere when I talked to her—not that that was a testament of innocence.

I sighed to myself. I felt that I had taken a big step the first day on the job, but from there on in my work was really cut out for me. There were a lot of things to find out, and no place to start. I probably had the starting point for the arsonists, but they were not going to be easy either. About the only thing I could do with them was push them until something cracked. But in the meantime I had to find all the other answers about Richard Cantwell, Pamela Cantwell, and Kayoko Asakura. It was a big order.

I finished the martini and decided that I'd better go to my room and get ready for my date. I looked longingly at the gin and vermouth back of the bar, and then exerted my will power. I paid the check and left the bar.

The Pacific-Melton Hotel is the sort you often find in semi-tropical climates. There were rooms in the main building, but then there were additional rooms that were small bungalows scattered over the grounds around the main building. Mine was one of the latter. I walked outside, skirted the kidney-shaped swimming pool, and made my way to the bungalow that I was temporarily calling home. I unlocked the door and stepped inside. I found the light switch and snapped the lights on. Then I closed the door and turned back to the room, taking my coat off. I stopped with the coat halfway down my back. I wasn't entirely alone. There was a girl stretched out on the couch, her head propped up on one hand. She was pretty, young, and had the most startling red hair I had ever seen. It was long and wavy, falling down over her shoulders. But it didn't fall far enough.

She was naked. Not a stitch of clothes anywhere. Her body was as beautiful as the rest of her, the breasts full and firm, the legs long and tapering, the belly a slight oval the way it should be.

She was beautiful, as I said, but that wasn't what had stopped me. I had seen beautiful women before. I'd also seen naked women before. But as well as I could remember, this was the first time I'd ever found a beautiful, naked woman in my room who was also holding a gun. And the gun was pointed unwaveringly at me.

FIVE

You might have thought we were posing for an old-fashioned photograph. We stayed frozen in the same positions for several seconds while we stared at each other—although I was doing more looking than she was. There was a little smile on her face as though she were enjoying the sensation she had created.

"Hello," she said. Her voice was low and husky.

"Hello," I said. "I hate to mention it, but I think one of us must have made a mistake and gotten into the wrong room."

"You're Milo March?"

"Yes."

"Then there's no mistake, honey. Take off your things and make yourself comfortable."

"I suppose I should be flattered," I said slowly, "but I'm afraid somebody has been telling you the wrong things about me. It's never been necessary for a beautiful woman to pull a gun on me in order to get me to make a pass."

"You are a pretty attractive hunk of man," she said. "It's too bad we don't have about a week for fun and games."

"Well, we'll just have to crowd it all into one night," I said. I was talking off the top of my head, stalling for time and trying to figure out what this was all about. "In the meantime, why don't you put the gun away and we can start getting acquainted." I took a step toward her.

"Don't try it, honey. Just stay across the room and do what I tell you."

"What I had in mind will be a little difficult from across the room."

"We'll manage." She waved the gun to emphasize her next words. "Stay where you are and get undressed."

"Undressed?"

She nodded. "Every stitch, honey. And don't try any tricks. I'm a very good shot. Under the circumstances, I could probably get away with shooting you."

"You probably could," I admitted. I started to undress slowly, still trying to figure out what the hell was going on. "Do you always carry a gun when you're in the nude?"

"Only when I think it's necessary."

"Do you have a permit for that gun?"

"No, but you do," she said.

I took a closer look, and she was right. It was my gun she was holding.

"That's adding insult to injury," I said. "When are you going to tell me what this is all about?"

"Soon enough. Stop stalling. Get your clothes off." Even moving as slowly as I could, there came a time when the last of my clothes were off and I stood there naked—and feeling it. I don't know why, but a man feels even more defenseless without his clothes. It shouldn't make any difference when you're facing a gun, but it does.

"Do you mind if I have a cigarette?" I asked. "And maybe a drink?"

"Go ahead," she said. "You can pour a drink for me, too. I

already helped myself to one, but I'll have another."

I got a cigarette from my shirt pocket and lit it. I got the bottle of V.O. that I had in the room, and found the second glass. I walked over toward her.

"Take it easy, honey," she said. "Don't get any ideas that you can take the gun away from me. And don't make any sudden moves, or I'll shoot first and ask the questions later. By then you may not be able to hear them."

I poured her a generous drink and retreated. I poured one for myself and sat in a chair across the room from her. "You have two advantages on me," I told her. "First, you're pointing my own gun at me. Second, you know my name, but I don't know yours."

"My friends call me Torchy."

"What's all of it?"

"Uh-uh," she said. "That's all you need for now. If you don't get reckless, you may be around to read the rest of it in the newspapers tomorrow morning."

"A celebrity?" I asked in mock surprise. "I always like to meet celebrities. What are you, the recording secretary for the Sun Bathers of California, or maybe the recruiting sergeant?"

She laughed. It was a nice laugh, but I was beginning to get the idea that she was on the sick side, and not just because she was holding my gun in such a professional manner. "It's too bad that you're a job," she said. "You might be fun. Tell me, had you been drinking before you reached here?"

"A few. I had a couple for breakfast. Then four or five in the early afternoon, and a martini in the hotel bar, just before I came over. Why?"

"Finish your drink and have another."

I tossed off the drink in my glass. "You're so generous with my liquor, Torchy. How about you?"

"Sure," she said. She finished her drink and pushed the glass across the end table. "But don't get any ideas of drinking me under the table. It's been tried by better men than you."

I went over and got the bottle. "I'm sure it's been tried," I said, "but I wouldn't be too sure they were better men." I poured the drinks, moving carefully when I went to get her glass. Sick she might be, but I had an idea she was telling the truth about the shooting.

She laughed again. "Like I say, it's too bad you're a job. I like you, Milo."

"And I like you, Torchy," I said seriously. "What kind of a job am I?"

"I'll tell you, but first come over here."

I got up and walked over to the couch. She reached up and put the muzzle of the gun against my ribs. The steel was cold and I could feel my skin trying to crawl away from it.

"Lean over—carefully," she said, "and kiss me."

What can you do with a gun in your side? I leaned over and kissed her. I hadn't really expected much, but her mouth was warm and inviting, and I found it turning into the real thing. Then suddenly, she reached up with her left hand and pushed against my chest. As I stepped back, her fingers curled and her nails raked down. It stung, and I automatically started a swing with my right hand, but the barrel of the gun sank a full inch into my belly and I stopped. She laughed.

"That's right, honey," she said, "take it easy."

I glanced down at my chest. There were four thin streaks of blood from my collarbone almost to my navel. "What the hell was the idea of that?" I asked. "You get your kicks that way?"

"Go back and sit down," she ordered. She waited until I was back in the chair. "I was right about you, honey. That was quite a kiss. If we had that week together, you might put a match to me. If you really behave, maybe we can try it sometime."

"Why not now?" I asked. My chest was burning, but I ignored it.

"I told you I'm working," she said. "But if you're a good boy, you'll live through it, and then we'll see."

"You still haven't told me what you're working at," I reminded her. "In the meantime, your lipstick is smeared."

"That's the way I want it to be, honey. That's part of the job, too."

I looked at her and waited. I knew then that she was going to tell me and that there was no point in pushing. Once she told me, maybe I could figure out the next move.

"You're trouble for some friends of mine," she said. "They sent me around to take care of it."

"What kind of trouble?" I asked.

"Too much snooping," she answered, shaking her head until the red hair danced. "You had a busy day, little man, running around, and asking questions, and snooping into things that aren't any of your business. I'm here to see that you stop."

I looked at her curiously. "You mean you work for Harry Manfred?"

"I didn't say who I worked for. I only said that you're bothering some friends of mine."

I leaned back and laughed. "You mean the great Harry Manfred has finally gotten around to using a female gunslinger? What's wrong with those two fancy hoods who were with him today? They can't handle things anymore?"

"They're all right," she said coolly, "but I work smarter. Is it really true that you're not for sale?"

"I don't know. I might be. But I don't think you or Harry Manfred could afford the price. Where does that leave us?"

"Right where we started. How about another round of drinks?"

"All right." I got up and poured the drinks, again making them stiff ones. If the bottle held out, maybe she wouldn't.

"I don't want to kill you," she said when I was back in the chair. "And my friends don't want you killed. It's bad for business. That doesn't mean that I won't kill you if I have to."

"So far," I said, "all I've offered you is a fate worse than death. So where does that leave us?"

"I'm going to tell you," she said. "That'll make it more fun as it works out. I'm going to fix you, honey, so that nobody in this town will give you the time of the day. It's much better than killing you—especially since it saves you for another day and another kind of job."

"How are you going to fix me?" I asked.

"It's easy. Here we are in your hotel room, both of us stripped right down to the buff. Pretty soon I'm going to start screaming. When somebody arrives, they will find the two of us here, naked. You with scratches on your chest and me with your gun, protecting my honor. If they test us, they'll find a lot of alcohol in both of us. My story will be that you picked me up and brought me here, then fed me a lot of liquor. I passed out and when I came to, I found that you had undressed me and yourself and were trying to attack me. I fought you off, screaming, and then grabbed your gun. It's a simple, straight-forward story—and it'll work."

It probably would, too, I thought, but I wasn't going to admit it out loud. "Why make it a frame?" I asked. "Why not let me be guilty and have a little pleasure out of it?"

"I never mix fun and work, honey," she said. "You'll be arrested tonight, but when it comes to court I'll refuse to press the charges, so nothing serious will happen to you. But it ought to make the front pages of all the newspapers."

She certainly had a point there. All the papers would do was take one look at her, and that would ensure its making page one. An insurance detective would help to make it a good spicy story. And she was right about something else: it would finish me in Los Angeles and maybe in other spots, too. At least, until people had a chance to forget the story. I could just imagine the expression on Martin Raymond's face when he saw the story. And I could imagine how many jobs I'd get out of him after that. I think it was the sudden vision of no more hundred-dollars-a-day-and-expenses jobs that made me realize that I'd better think of something.

"It's nice of you not to press charges," I said dryly. "You know you'd never make it all the way through a trial."

"Of course not, honey," she said cheerfully. "But I don't have to. All I have to do is make sure the newspapers get a good story, and that it's on the police squeal books long enough for the reporters to get it. After that, I just fade out of the picture and there's no charge against you."

"Your solicitude touches me. Are you going to pose for the papers the way you are now?"

She smiled. "I wouldn't mind. But by the time they get to me I'll be dressed again—in a demure little dress that's just right for the job."

"You do think of everything," I murmured. "What if somebody gets curious and looks up your record?"

"I don't have one, honey. Little Torchy is smart. That's why I do all right. Like this job. The way of handling it is my own idea. My friends wanted to give you some rough stuff, but from what I hear about you, that wouldn't work with you. This will, because there isn't anything you can do about it."

"I have to admit that it's smart," I said. I stood up. "How about another drink?"

"Sure," she said. "I like the stuff. And another one ought to make it certain that we both score well on the balloon test, in case any bright cop wants to check my story. But remember what I said—don't get any ideas."

"The only idea I have," I protested as I moved to the bottle, "is the one you've ruled out until later." I picked up the bottle and moved in the direction of the couch, the point of the gun following me as I went. "Are you a Native Daughter, Torchy?"

"No. I'm from the big town, the same as you."

"What if I offered to pay you more than your friends are paying you?"

"No dice, honey. I like money, but once I've made a deal, I stick to it."

"I was afraid of that," I sighed. I reached the end table and poured her a good-sized drink. This time I'd carried my own glass with me and I filled it, then put the bottle down on the end table. "If you'd only let me put on my pants ... there are such a limited number of things a man can do well without any clothes at all." She laughed as I thought she would. I held my glass in my left hand and picked up her glass with my right. "Well, at least, let's drink a toast to the next meeting you mentioned."

"All right," she said, "but remember—nothing funny."

"Nothing funny," I said seriously.

She propped herself up higher on her left elbow so that she could take the glass in her left hand. The gun was steady in her right hand. I handed her the glass, moving slowly so she wouldn't think I was up to anything. She took it and I switched my glass to my right hand. I leaned down so that I could clink my glass with hers, which was close to her face because of the awkward position of her body on the couch. Her warm scent floated up to caress my senses.

"I like you, honey," she said. "We'll have a ball when this is all over."

"Sure, we will," I said. "Here's to the way the ball is going to bounce."

Then just as the two glasses were about to touch, I shoved mine forward and upward as hard as I could. The glasses hit with a sharp crack, the liquor from both exploding up into her face. At the same time, I twisted to one side and chopped down blindly with my left hand. The gun exploded about the same time. I was vaguely aware of a burning sensation on my left shoulder and the sound of a vague thud back of me.

Her reactions were fast. The liquor must have half blinded her, but with a single fluid motion she was swinging to her feet and bringing the gun back into line. I was ready for that, too. I had already dropped my glass. I swung my right as hard as I could, right at the point of her jaw. It was a good blow; I could feel it all the way to my shoulder. Her face went slack and she sagged back on the couch. The gun dropped to the floor.

I stared at her for a minute, just trying to get my breath back to normal, thankful that I'd had some luck. Then I became conscious of my left shoulder again. I glanced down at it. There was a red crease about an inch long. But the blood was only seeping from it, so it wasn't too serious. I looked around the room and finally saw the hole in the plaster of one wall.

I bent over and picked up my gun. Then I looked at the girl. She was unconscious and looked as if she'd be out for a few minutes. I put away my gun and got dressed as fast as I could. I'd just finished tying my shoes when the phone rang. I picked it up and said hello.

"Mr. March," a man's voice said, "this is the desk clerk. Is there anything wrong in your bungalow?"

"My goodness," I said, "you people must be telepathic. I was having a little trouble with one of the lights, but it's nothing very serious. I certainly appreciate—"

"Was there a gunshot in your room?" he interrupted. "One of the guests just phoned and said he heard a gunshot there."

I gave my heartiest laugh. "That's pretty silly. I'm deathly afraid of guns. I'm afraid that it's that light I mentioned. One of the bulbs was out and I tried to switch bulbs and I'm afraid that I dropped it. It did make a rather loud noise."

"Oh, I see," he said with obvious relief. "I will reassure the guest and send a boy over to fix the lights at once."

"Just a minute," I said. "If you don't mind, I'm trying to get out to keep an appointment. I'd rather you sent the boy over in an hour or so, after I'm gone."

"Very well. I'm sorry I bothered you, Mr. March." He hung up.

I went to the door and looked out. There didn't seem to be anyone hovering around. It was dark and I was glad to see that the grounds weren't too well lighted. I went back into the room and found the girl's clothes. I carried them over to the couch and dressed her. It's quite a job to put clothes on a completely limp body, but I finally managed it. She probably wasn't dressed as neatly as she would have been if she'd done it herself, but it would serve the purpose. I lifted her eyelids and looked at her pupils. She was still out.

I picked up the bottle of V.O., gazed at it with regret, then poured what was left of it over her hair and dress. I checked the door again. There was nobody in sight. I turned out my lights, picked her up, and went outside. I scurried across a driveway and entered the parking lot. There were several cars there but nobody in sight. I found an Imperial that was unlocked and put her in the front seat. She was beginning to stir slightly as I left.

I went back to the bungalow and made sure the door was locked. I undressed and looked at my wound. It wasn't bleeding much. The bullet had only grazed the skin. I went into the bathroom and shaved and showered. The hot water stung my shoulder. When I'd finished, I put a Band-Aid on the crease and got dressed.

I looked at my watch. It was too late to call New York, but I could make my date. I went out to my car. On the way, I looked in the Imperial. She was gone. I got into the Cadillac and headed for Beverly Hills.

I was right on time when I rang the bell. The maid answered the ring and showed me into what was probably called a drawing room—although in my circles it would have been just a fancy living room. She said Mrs. Cantwell would be right down. I thought that probably meant I'd have to wait a half hour or more, but she surprised me. She came in five minutes later. She wore a black gown that hugged her figure with an almost human intensity. She looked like a million dollars—which was roughly what she might soon have.

"Hello," she said. "I hope I didn't keep you waiting long."

"I've never known a woman who was more prompt," I said. "And thank you for agreeing to see me tonight."

"It was the least I could do in the line of duty," she said lightly. "I thought we might have one drink here before we went out. I asked Elizabeth to make us two martinis. She makes them very well. I hope that is all right."

"Perfect. How'd you happen to settle on martinis?"

"I thought you looked like a martini man. Was I wrong?"

"As right as it's possible to be. I just didn't know that it showed."

The maid came in then with the two martinis. They were generous ones. From the feel of the glass I knew they had been chilled just right.

"Well," Pamela Cantwell said when the maid was gone,

"here's to crime. Isn't that the way you say it?" She lifted her glass.

"That's one way of saying it," I agreed seriously. I raised my glass to touch hers, thinking fleetingly of the last toast I had started to drink. "Here's to crime."

We drank. The martini was good, with just the hint of vermouth that turns gin into nectar fit for the gods.

"I thought that a fitting toast," she said. "After all, a crime has made me both a free and a rich woman. And even though it's not my crime, you'd like to pin it on me and save all that money. Wouldn't you?"

"That's not quite true," I told her. "I'd like to find out all of the answers, no matter where they fall. Anyway, you're not my first choice as a suspect."

"Who is?"

"Richard Cantwell."

"Nonsense. The body was identified beyond a shadow of a doubt. Shall we go?"

We went. We drove down Sunset Boulevard and stopped at one of the restaurants on it just before reaching Hollywood. It wasn't as famous as some of the other restaurants, but its food was unmatched. We had another martini and then dinner. Only once, while we were having coffee, did she bring the subject back to the case.

"Milo," she said—by then we were on a first-name basis— "why do you persist in thinking that Richard planned the fire and the two deaths in it?"

"Somebody planned it," I said. "We are certain that fire was set by professional arsonists brought out here from New

York. Somebody had to hire them and pay them. They cost a lot—usually a percentage of the policy. Now, there were only three possible places of gain in the case. You would collect if only your husband died, he would collect if only you died, and the foundation would collect if both of you died. Considering the caliber of the particular arsonists in this one, I'd say that they had to be hired by a beneficiary of the policies. I doubt if even your husband's worst enemy could afford the price that would have to be paid to them. And in the context of this theory, Richard Cantwell is by far the best possibility."

"Why?"

I decided not to tell her about the money that was missing from the business. She'd find out about that soon enough, anyway.

"Well, if both of you had died in the fire, or seemed to have, the foundation would collect. He set up the foundation and kept it going. So far as I know now, he was the only person in the foundation who might have worked out such a scheme. Then, considering the thoroughness of the identification of one body as that of Richard Cantwell, he was the only one who could have made such identification possible—unless it really was his body in the fire. In that case you would be the most logical suspect. But I think that he intended to have us believe that both of you died in that fire. Tell me, did he make any attempt to get you to visit the Santa Monica house in the last few days?"

She thought a minute, then looked surprised. "Yes, he did. When I told him that I was going to the mountain lodge with Debby, he tried to talk me out of it and suggested that we spend a few days in Santa Monica. It was so long since he'd suggested that we go anywhere together that I just laughed and forgot about it."

"That fits. Not having you available, he could have found a substitute for you as well as for himself. He could always kill you elsewhere if there had been a body in the fire that was identified as being yours."

"There's only one thing wrong with that," she said. "If you were right, someone should have tried to kill me."

"Maybe they did. Debby Vance told me that there was an avalanche that almost caught the two of you while you were skiing one day. Avalanches can be started by someone."

She looked startled. "I'd forgotten about that. It just seemed to be the sort of thing that happens once in a while. You think it might have been started by ... someone?" She was staring at me thoughtfully.

"Yes."

"And do you think Richard might still be alive somewhere?"

"I do."

She shivered. "I hope you're wrong," she said fervently. "I won't lie to you, Milo. I don't know when I've felt such relief as when I heard Richard was dead. It may be a terrible thing to say, but it's true. ... Do you think he—if he's still alive—might try again to kill me?"

"I doubt it. He would probably know that it's too late. I would assume that you have already taken certain steps to change things so that the money wouldn't go to the foundation now even if you did die. I imagine he would assume the same thing. No, if I'm right, he'll be more apt to show up later and demand a hefty cut of what you collect—possibly on the threat of involving you if you turn him in."

Her face was pale. "I can only hope you're wrong. Please, let's talk about something else."

"I didn't bring it up," I said, but I switched the conversation to another subject. We finished our coffee and then went to a nightclub in Hollywood. She shook off her depression and we had a good time. I finally took her back to Beverly Hills about midnight. She asked me in for a nightcap and I accepted. The nightcap stretched into a couple of hours. I had a little trouble explaining the scratches on my chest and the Band-Aid on my shoulder.

It was about two in the morning when I got back to my hotel. This time my room was empty. I went straight to bed and was asleep five minutes after my head hit the pillow.

It was almost nine o'clock when I awakened the next morning. I called room service and ordered breakfast: ham and eggs, toast, and a pot of coffee. I took a quick shower and shave while I waited for the order to be delivered. The waiter arrived shortly after I came out of the bathroom. I added a tip to the check and signed it. I reached for the telephone and put in a person-to-person call to Lieutenant Johnny Rockland on the New York City Police Force.

Finally the operator told me to go ahead.

"Hi, Johnny," I said. "This is Milo March."

"What are you doing in California?" he asked.

"Working on a case. But this is only the second day, so I don't know how it's going yet."

"And I suppose you just called me to say hello. You don't happen to want something or anything like that?"

"As a matter of fact, I do," I said cheerfully. "It's about somebody you might know."

"Who?"

"I don't know her real name," I said. "I'd say she's in her late twenties, about five six or seven, weight a hundred and twenty. If I haven't lost my eye for such things, her measurements must be about 36-24-36. She has flaming red hair and she's a knockout, no matter what angle you look from. Her friends, I'm told, call her Torchy. And she's from New York. That's all I have."

He was silent for a couple of seconds. "Boy, when you decide to get involved with someone, you really pick them, don't you? Where'd you run into her?"

"In my hotel room. When I came back last evening she was in the room, without any clothes on, and pointing my own gun at me."

He laughed. "I wondered how you were able to be so accurate about the measurements. That I would like to have seen. Well, she doesn't have a record—but not because we haven't tried to give her one—if that's what you want to know."

"I'd like to know a little more," I said mildly.

"You always do. Somebody might think from the way you act that the New York Police was your own private force. Well, her real names is Lillian Cassidy. She used to be called Lil until they started calling her Torchy. She works for Harry Manfred and has since she was nineteen, which was about eight years ago."

"I thought she was hooked up with him in some way. He's out here, too."

"I knew he was, but I didn't know about her. What's the case, Milo?"

"Arson and murder."

"Manfred is an expert in both fields, all right. Think you can pin it on him?"

"I don't know, but I'm hoping."

"I'm with you, son. Who's the L.A. cop on the case?"

"Lieutenant Frank Arnold."

"I don't know him, I guess. But they've got a good department out there. You'll do us a favor here if you can get Manfred. He's pretty far up the ladder."

"I know all about that. I didn't call you to find out about Manfred. What about the girl? What does she do for him?"

"All I can give you, Milo, are the guesses, because we've never succeeded in pinning anything on her. She first started working for him when he was still in the call-girl business. She rode herd on the string of girls—and rode them hard, from everything I've heard. She must have done a good job, because she's moved along with Manfred wherever he went. Now that he's organized the arson business, we think that she's a chief torch, and that's the reason she's called Torchy. We also think that she's done a few killings for him. She's real handy with a gun, just in case she ever gets the drop on you again. What was she going to do, kill you?"

"No. She made me undress, stuffed me with my own liquor, put a few nail scratches on my chest, then she was going to scream and claim that I plied her with liquor and tried to attack her when I thought she had passed out. She was even honest about the reason. She said her friends didn't like me snooping around on the case I'm on. She figured her little scheme would get enough newspaper publicity to cripple my investigation."

"It probably would have, too. How'd you get out of it?"

"Threw a drink in her face and slugged her on the jaw. I collected a burned shoulder and a hole in the wall of the room, but that's all. I don't understand one thing. Intercontinental Insurance has a file on Manfred and arson, including most of his men, but there's no mention of her in it. And I never heard of a female torch before."

"Well, you have now. And it just goes to show that the insurance companies don't know everything. They've got a bunch of clucks working for them—present company excluded, of course."

"It's a good thing you added that," I said. "I can think of a few cases I could ram down your throat. Well, I'll keep in touch."

"You do that. Happy hunting, Milo." He hung up.

I put the phone down and ate my breakfast. I lingered over my coffee for fifteen or twenty minutes, then got dressed and left. My first stop was the police department. Lieutenant Arnold saw me immediately.

"Hello, March," he said. "Did you come in to hand us the solution to the case?"

"Not yet," I said. "It's too early in the morning. Besides, I thought you might have it all wrapped up by this time."

"We're making progress," he said placidly. "What's on your mind?"

"I'm checking up on that cooperation," I said. "I want some information."

"What kind?"

"The name of the dentist who made the identification in the case of Richard Cantwell."

"It was his personal dentist, so you could get it from anybody who knew him. It was Dr. Samuel Beach in Beverly Hills."

"Thanks," I said. I looked at him. "Making any headway with identifying the body of the woman?"

"Not yet. But we will."

"I suppose you've checked with the Missing Persons Bureau?"

"Gee," he said sarcastically, "I don't know what I'd do without your cooperation, March. I'll make a note of it."

"As long as you don't write the note in my blood, I don't mind. You know, Lieutenant, I just had a funny thought. How come you're on this case at all?"

"What kind of a crack is that supposed to be?" he demanded.

"No crack. The fire and the murder happened in Santa Monica. I thought that was a separate town, not part of Los Angeles. So how come you're involved?"

"You know the old joke," he said. "The city limits of Los Angeles are just outside of Chicago. Actually, this is a funny territory. We have a strip between Hollywood and Beverly Hills that is out of our jurisdiction, then there's a section along the ocean, beyond Santa Monica limits, which is part of our jurisdiction. Cantwell's house was in that area."

"I'm glad to know that you're legal, Lieutenant," I said with a smile. "Any idea yet who put the match to the house?"

"No. It must have been one of the men who are here with Harry Manfred, but we have nothing that pins it on one of them. Whichever one it was, he was a professional. We'll dig him out."

"How many people are here with Manfred?" I asked.

"So far as we know at the moment, there are two guys with him. One named Hale, the other Warren. Manfred claims that one is his secretary and the other his valet."

"That's all?"

"Yes."

"What about women with him?"

"No women with him. He's been seeing some local girls— all professionals—but he didn't bring any with him. Why?"

"Just curious," I said. I'd decided that I wouldn't tell the lieutenant about Torchy just yet. "Maybe the torch is local talent."

He shook his head. "I don't think so. We checked out all the known ones in the area and they are all accounted for during the time involved. Besides, I don't think the ones we have are that good. So it must be either Hale or Warren."

"Could be," I admitted. "Tell me, Lieutenant, do you have a theory about this case?"

He stared at me for at least a full minute before he answered. Then he apparently made up his mind. "You might say so, but it's not for publication. Cantwell was, if you'll excuse the expression, something of a sonofabitch. I think that might be the motive. If we can identify the woman who was with him, I think we may then find out that she had either a boyfriend or a husband who did the job. Or it might turn out to be the boyfriend or husband of some other girl in the past, or a business enemy, and the present woman just happened to get caught in the same trap."

"It's a good theory," I said cautiously, "but there is a lot of money involved. When there's something like a million dollars at stake, I've usually discovered that the money fits in somehow with the crime. What about the wife?"

"She's covered for the time. Not just by her friend. We had the state police check it out. The two women went there just when they say they did and apparently stayed there until Tuesday."

"She could have done that and still be guilty. If you and I are right about Harry Manfred, all she had to do was hire him and then take off."

"Yeah," he said. "But we've checked that out as well as we can. There is no evidence that she ever had any contact with Manfred or anyone connected with him. We think she's in the clear."

"What about Cantwell himself?"

He stared at me. "What do you mean?"

"Maybe Cantwell found a ringer for the fire, and now he's sitting off someplace waiting to collect."

"You insurance dicks," he said with scorn, "have more imagination than those cop shows on television. How's he going to collect? From his wife? She hated his guts. Once she gets her hands on that money, her husband, even if he was alive, couldn't pry it loose from her with dynamite."

"Maybe. On the other hand, if he threatened to involve her if she didn't play along, she might figure it was better to end up with part of the money instead of none. Or Cantwell may have had some other plan in mind when he set the thing up."

"I don't know how you guys make out," he said, shaking his head. "You certainly reach. If we tried to run our investigations the way you run yours, we'd be out of business."

"Would that be bad?" I asked innocently and watched his face darken. "That was a joke, son. I permit myself one a day. Sorry you don't like the Cantwell theory, but such things have been known to happen."

"I know," he said sourly. "I've worked on a couple of them myself. When they do happen there's always some kind of evidence—not just the wishful thinking of some insurance company that wants to save money. Did you want anything else, March?"

"Not a thing," I said cheerfully. "I'll be seeing you, Lieutenant."

"Do that. Drop around when you get anything to support your theory. I'm still waiting to see some of your cooperation."

"You know I will, Lieutenant. I'm a civic-minded citizen." I gave him my best smile and departed.

Downstairs, I found a phone booth and called the Intercontinental office. I got the manager on the phone right away.

"I was waiting for your call," he said. "I've got the information you wanted. I thought you'd probably want it as soon as possible."

"Good," I said. "What is it?"

"The Japanese-American Cultural Corporation is a nonprofit corporation controlled by four persons. They are Kayoko Asakura, John Tamashiro, Benny Kishimoto, and Jason

Hotoyama. The last three constitute the board of directors, and Miss Asakura is designated as the director of the corporation."

"There's nobody else?"

"That's all."

"Know anything about the three men?"

"I thought you'd ask that. I have what we were able to dig up on short notice. All three of the men are second-generation Japanese-Americans. All three of them are successful businessmen with good ratings in Dun and Bradstreet. So far as we are able to find out on short notice, they are well thought of in business and financial circles."

"Do you have any local investigators?" I asked.

"Yes. Two men, but usually they work only on application investigations, so they haven't had much experience."

"Have one of them check on the three Japanese, especially to see if there's any connection between them and Cantwell. He doesn't have to be a Sherlock Holmes to do that. I'll handle the girl myself."

"All right. I'll put one of them on it right away."

I said I'd keep in touch and hung up. I got in the car and drove to Beverly Hills. The dentist's office was in a handsome, modern building just off Wilshire Boulevard. I parked the car and went up. The doctor's receptionist was a pretty brunette. She looked up and gave me a smile that was a good advertisement for a dentist. "I'd like to see Dr. Beach," I said.

"Do you have an appointment?"

"No. And I don't need my teeth fixed. But tell him I'd like to see him anyway."

"I—I don't understand."

"Tell him I want to talk to him about a late patient of his—Richard Cantwell."

She got up and left the room. She was back a minute later. "You may go in there," she said, indicating another door. "He'll be with you as soon as he can."

I opened the door and stepped into a regular treatment room. There weren't any other chairs, so I sat in the dental chair. I lit a cigarette and used the water bowl as an ashtray.

I didn't have long to wait. The door opened and he came in. He was probably in his late fifties, with a well-groomed, prosperous look about him. He probably had a great chairside manner when he was with a patient, but he was frowning when he looked at me.

"I don't understand what this is about," he said abruptly.

"It's easy," I told him. "My name is Milo March. I represent the insurance company that issued all of Mr. Cantwell's policies. I'd like to ask you a few questions."

He looked even more irritated. "Why? I gave a complete report to the police. That should be sufficient."

"Not for me. In the first place, I don't have access to all the police reports. Besides, I might want to ask some questions which I suspect they didn't."

"I'm a very busy man. If you'll make it brief ... what did you say your name was?"

"Milo March. Richard Cantwell was your patient, wasn't he?"

"Yes. For more than ten years."

"Mrs. Cantwell, too?"

"She came twice a year for a cleaning, but that was all. She has perfect teeth, not a cavity in her mouth."

"That was also true of the woman found in the fire?"

"Yes. For that reason, I could not say whether it was Mrs. Cantwell or not."

"But it was different in the case of Richard Cantwell?"

"Yes. He'd had very extensive work, so it was comparatively easy to identify him."

"You're certain that the identification was right?"

"Absolutely," he snapped.

"Did you make it on the basis of anything other than his teeth?"

"No. There wasn't much left except bones and teeth. But I didn't need anything else. Everything in those teeth matched Mr. Cantwell's Xrays perfectly."

"No chance of error?"

"None."

"Let me ask you something else, Doctor. Did Mr. Cantwell ever bring you a patient and ask you to do work for him that was quite similar to what had been done for him?"

He looked at me in amazement. "Of course not. Mr. Cantwell was not an expert on dentistry. He sent a few patients to me over the years, but he certainly never presumed to tell me what should be done for them. I wouldn't have listened if he had."

"Did you like Richard Cantwell?" I asked.

He gave me a wintry smile. "It is not necessary in my profession to either like or dislike my patients. I probably wouldn't know many of them if I met them on the street—unless they opened their mouths."

I looked around the room. "Where do you keep the Xrays? In here?"

"In here and there's another cabinet of them in the next office," he said impatiently.

"You mean half the alphabet in here and half in there?" I asked. I didn't really care. I was just trying to stall until I could think of something else to ask.

"No. There's a complete file in here. Those in the other room are duplicates."

"You keep duplicates of all your Xrays?"

"Yes." He made a point of glancing at his watch, but I ignored this.

"Why?"

"In case of fire. Or sometimes a new girl may mislay an Xray. I find it more efficient to keep two sets for each patient. It's a way of avoiding possible trouble."

"It sounds like a very good system," I said. I was trying to think of some way Cantwell could have taken advantage of the fact that his dentist had duplicate Xrays.

"So you have two copies of Richard Cantwell's Xrays?"

"No."

It was my turn to be surprised. "No? I thought you said you always made duplicates."

"I do. I didn't say that I had all the duplicates. About forty or fifty of them are missing, and have been ever since the theft."

I felt the first stirring of excitement. "What theft?"

"Someone broke in here," he said, "two or three months ago. They took what money was here, a few tools, and forty or fifty Xrays. The duplicate Xrays of Richard Cantwell were among those taken."

SIX

For a full minute I stared at him, letting his last words sink in. I had come there on a fishing expedition and it felt as if I'd had a strike. I hadn't had anything special to ask and hadn't really expected too much. Then, just as I was ready to leave, he had volunteered something I would never have thought of asking for. Investigations are often like that, which is one of the reasons I like my work.

He looked at his watch again. "Well, Mr. March—"

"Just a minute," I said, "and then I'll let you get back to work. When did you say this theft took place?"

"Two or three months ago."

"What happened?"

"Someone broke in here at night," he said impatiently. "They took the petty cash that was in my receptionist's desk, a few of my tools—nothing very valuable—and a handful of Xrays. That's all."

"How'd they get in?"

"Broke the lock on the door. The police said that it looked like an amateurish job. Probably some kids, maybe high on drugs."

"You have drugs here. Did they take any?"

"No. But maybe they couldn't find them."

"The police ever catch them?"

"No. Of course, there wasn't much to go on. The police didn't find any fingerprints or anything like that. The thieves probably threw the tools away and destroyed the Xrays."

"Why do you say that?"

"That's what the police thought. They figured that the thieves only took the tools and the Xrays out of spite, because there was so little money. There was only about three dollars in the drawer that night."

"Thank you, Dr. Beach," I said. "I won't bother you anymore. You've just made me a happy man."

He looked at me as if he thought I'd suddenly lost my mind, then turned on his heel and went back the way he had come. I went out of the room, smiled at the pretty brunette, and left.

I headed toward downtown L.A. I felt there were still answers there and what I had just learned made me more anxious to get on with it. Of course, it wasn't anything definite enough to take to the police or even to a court, but I felt it was something. It was interesting that Dr. Beach's office had been broken into and the Xrays, including those of Cantwell, stolen at about the same time that Cantwell was floating around Skid Row and getting chummy with a bum. I don't believe in coincidences. And there was something else in what the dentist had said. The door to his office had been forced as though by an amateur, according to the police, but whoever had broken in had been smart enough not to leave any prints.

Maybe I was reaching, but it sounded to me like someone like Cantwell. He would be an amateur at breaking locks, but he would also be smart enough not to leave any fingerprints.

And I didn't buy the police version of the crime as given by Dr. Beach. If it had been hopped-up kids looking for money to buy drugs, then they certainly would have looked for drugs when they found themselves in a doctor's office. And if they'd looked, there would have been evidence of a search. Also, if it had been kids who were angry because there wasn't more money, they would have destroyed things in the office—not just taken a few worthless tools and Xrays. No, the more I thought about it, the more I believed that somebody had taken the petty cash and the tools to cover the fact that all they wanted were the Xrays. Or in this case, one set of Xrays.

But I still had to find the answers to a lot of questions. If Cantwell had picked up a bum to substitute for him in the fire, where and by whom were the teeth fixed? Who was the girl in the fire? Why was she there? Was she meant to be taken for Pamela Cantwell while the latter was killed elsewhere? Had Cantwell hired Manfred to set the fire? If so, how had he gotten in touch with Manfred? How did someone in Los Angeles, who was supposedly an honest businessman, get in touch with the king of arsonists?

I was still mentally going over these questions when I became aware of something tugging at my mind. It took me a few seconds to realize what it was. Finally I made it. There was a car behind me and I had noticed it at least twice before that same day. It was a gray Oldsmobile convertible. I had noticed it behind me once on the way in from Santa Monica and once in Beverly Hills. I couldn't make out the driver, but somebody was following me. I didn't make any attempt to lose him. It was either the cops, which was all right, or somebody who worked for Manfred. That was all right, too. It would only push them a little more.

Since I was going to be in the neighborhood anyway, I stopped first at Cantwell's offices. I asked for Mr. Patman and was soon shown into his office. He greeted me with the air of a man who had just been beaten.

"What's the matter with you?" I asked. "You look as if you'd had a bad night."

"I did, Mr. March," he said seriously. "I was up almost all night going over the records. After what I told you yesterday, I thought it imperative that I make an effort either to verify or refute it."

"What did you find?"

"It will take a few more days to find the exact amount, but I can tell you that something slightly in excess of five hundred and fifty thousand dollars has been embezzled from this company."

"How much in excess?"

"I can't really say. Perhaps four or five hundred, maybe even a thousand."

"Well, that's close enough," I said. "You're sure that no one except Cantwell could have taken the money?"

"Positive. He was the only person who could sign checks or make withdrawals from the bank. I suppose that I shouldn't have said embezzled. Mr. Cantwell was the only stockholder and I don't suppose one can embezzle from oneself. But I don't understand why he did it this way. Why didn't he just take the money out in the usual way as profit? I've been trying to think of the answers, Mr. March. Taxes couldn't have been the reason, because there wouldn't have been any way to conceal the withdrawals from the tax men."

"If he'd taken the money out in a normal fashion, somebody would have had to know about it. At least you would have known. Isn't that true?"

He nodded his head, one hand fumbling at his glasses. "That is true. There would have had to be book entries. But why hide it from me? And how could he have spent that much money in such a short period of time?"

"It might be easy," I said. "Did you find out how he did it?"

"Oh, yes. I spoke to the bank. It was very easy. He merely went into the bank on different occasions and withdrew the money, using a counter check instead of a regular check. It was perfectly legal, but that way it did not show on the check stubs, so I knew nothing about it."

"What about the bank statements?"

"When those came in, Mr. Cantwell always took them. He kept them until he wanted me to bring the books up to date—which was usually twice a year. Every six months, in other words."

"Isn't that an unusual practice?"

"In most offices, yes. But Mr. Cantwell always operated in that fashion. I used to complain, since it made my work much harder, but it availed me nothing, so I finally accepted it."

"He probably played some hanky-panky before—when he had a partner," I said. "Well, you keep digging, Mr. Patman, and let me know of anything you dig up."

"But that isn't all," he said. "It may not be important, but while I was talking to the bank I received some additional information. Mr. Cantwell also kept his personal account there. Up until last Friday the balance in that account was always about a hundred and fifty thousand dollars. On Friday Mr. Cantwell withdrew all but fifty dollars. It was so unusual that one of the bank officials came out to ask him about it. He said that he had an important deal on over the weekend that would require a lot of cash."

"Well, at least we don't have that insured," I said. "Tell me, when the withdrawals were made from the company account, were those amounts deposited in his private account?"

"Apparently not. As a matter of fact, all of the withdrawals, including the one from his personal account, consisted entirely of bills of very large denomination."

"Do you happen to know if the bank made a note of the serial numbers?"

"I believe they did. All of this, however, was money to which Mr. Cantwell had a right, so I fail to see what good the serial numbers can do you." Suddenly the frown left his face. "Oh, I see. You think someone may have stolen the money before Mr. Cantwell died in the fire, and the numbers would help to catch him."

"Let's just say that I'm curious about where the money will turn up," I said. "I imagine that we can get the numbers from the bank. Thank you, Mr. Patman. You've been a big help."

"I only did what I thought was right," he said.

"I'm sure you did," I told him. "I'll see you again soon." I left.

Leaving the Cadillac parked where it was, I walked down the street and turned the corner. I looked into the bar where

I'd been the day before. Hank was there, seated at the bar. I went in and took the stool next to him. The bartender came over and I ordered some V.O. At the sound of my voice, Hank looked around.

"Ah," he said, "my benefactor of yesterday." He lifted the glass in front of him as the bartender gave me mine. " 'While you live, drink,' sir—'for once dead you never shall return.' "

I lifted my own glass and drank. "Let's hope that it doesn't happen too soon."

" 'The worldly hope men set their hearts upon turns ashes.' "

"You seem to be full of the *Rubaiyat* today," I said. "What happened to our friend Christopher Marlowe?"

"A matter of mood, sir. When I am full of what Omar calls the 'juice,' I sometimes prefer his Eastern philosophy. Although he does not have the rolling eloquence of him who died because of a 'great reckoning in a little room.' It's all a matter of moods."

"Are you often subject to moods?" I asked.

"Only since I took the daughter of the vine to spouse."

"We'll drink to the lady," I said. I beckoned the bartender and indicated our two empty glasses. He filled them up and took my money.

"As I believe I have remarked before," Hank said, "you are a gentleman of surpassing charm. I drink to you, sir." He drank and regarded the glass reflectively. " 'Why, be this juice the growth of God, who dare blaspheme the twisted tendril as a snare?' " He put the glass on the bar and looked at me. "I was giving some thought to trying to reach you when you walked in."

"Really?" I said in some surprise. I had just come to the conclusion that Hank had probably spent all of his time right at this bar since I had left money for him with the bartender.

"My only hesitation, sir, was caused by the need for some masterly approach to yonder foul innkeeper to get him to part with a dime of your benevolence of yesterday so that I could call you."

"You mean you have some news for me about Jimmy?"

"A modicum of news. I am not certain of its value, but it represents the results of my efforts in your behalf."

"Did you find out his name?"

"No. No names. It is futile to ask in this harem of the daughter of the vine. It would be even more futile to believe a name were it told to you. A hair perhaps divides the false and the true."

"All right," I said. "What did you find?"

"There is a building on the next street over, in the world beyond, which was visited daily by Jimmy from the time he began talking to the gentleman you asked about until the last time Jimmy was seen. Since the building harbors neither vintners nor cheap beds, I cannot imagine what he was doing there."

"What kind of building?"

"Offices. Where myriads scurry about the senseless tasks of that other world, seemingly unaware that yesterday this day's madness did prepare."

"What's the address?" I asked.

He shrugged. "Numbers—unless it be the number of drinks available—have as little meaning here as do names. I did not make note of the address."

"Will you take me to it, then?"

"Not necessary. If you walk to the next street and turn left, you cannot miss it. The street is full of shops except for this one building of offices."

"How'd you find out about it?"

"It seems that when it appeared that Jimmy had come into some money, one of our local citizens noticed him going off every day and followed him a few times, thinking that he might find the source of Jimmy's affluence."

"Did he find out where Jimmy went in the building?"

"No. I believe he tried, but wherever he asked questions he was hurriedly ejected. He soon lost his enthusiasm for the project."

"Who was this fellow?" I asked.

"Muskie. It's a cognomen of his own invention and is, I believe, derived from the one love of his life—Muscatel."

"Could I see him?"

"Not at the moment, I fear. Muskie was in the midst of a temporary prosperity when I talked to him last night and shortly afterwards fell victim to his own thirst. He was lying on the sidewalk outside, from whence he was plucked like a discarded blossom by the custodians of our freedom."

"Cops?"

He nodded.

"How soon will he be out, do you think?"

"It depends on the benevolence of the judge. But it doesn't matter. He told me all that he knew."

"Well, I'll go take a look," I said. "How are your reserves here holding up?"

"Still ample, sir. I resisted the temptation to partake of the more expensive distillations. As I believe I told you, the only important numbers are those which indicate the future drinks. I have worked it out minutely. By a careful nursing of my assets, I calculate that this will not be a depressed area until after tomorrow night."

"Good," I said. "I'll probably see you tomorrow or the next day, and we'll see what we can do about it."

"Tomorrow?" he said. " 'Why, tomorrow I may be myself with yesterday's seven thousand years.' "

"I'll keep it in mind," I said and left. Outside, I decided to leave the car where it was. I walked one block and was suddenly, as Hank had said, in another world. I wondered, as I turned left, if there was any symbolism to the fact that the main part of Skid Row ran between two streets of commerce.

The office building was easy to find. There were two department stores, a couple of clothing stores, and a large jewelry store on the street. Tucked in among them was a modern three-story office building. I went in and started to check. In each office I asked about Jimmy. I didn't have much of a description but fortunately didn't need much. If anyone like Jimmy had been around regularly, it would be remembered even a few months later. I drew a blank every place. But there were two offices I had to miss. One was a doctor's office and a sign on the door said he would be there at twelve o'clock. The other office belonged to a dentist and his sign said the office would be open at one-thirty. My money was on the dentist, so I'd be sure to get back in time.

I went back to the car and started uptown. I checked the

rearview mirror. Sure enough, I was being followed. I smiled and kept on going. It wasn't long before I pulled in to the curb and parked near the police building I wanted. I went in and found the Missing Persons Bureau on the directory. It was on the second floor. I told them what I wanted and was finally shown in to see a Lieutenant Howard, who sat at a desk in a large room with a lot of other plainclothesmen.

"What can I do for you?" he asked, automatically reaching for a form on his desk.

"You won't need the form," I said. "My name is Milo March. I work for Intercontinental Insurance. We're interested in that fire and double death out at the Santa Monica beach. You've heard about it?"

"I've heard about it," he said. Then he waited.

"The police believe they have identified the man—Richard Cantwell. At first, they thought the woman was his wife, but now we know that she wasn't. It occurred to me that the best place to start trying to find out who she was might be here in the Missing Persons Bureau."

"A good idea," he said. "Lieutenant Arnold also thought of it."

"I'm glad to hear that he's efficient. Do you mind telling me whatever you told him?"

"Not at all," he said cheerfully. "As I gathered from Lieutenant Arnold, the idea would be to find a girl who disappeared probably within twenty-four hours of the crime. That is, prior to it. I don't imagine that you're interested in those who had been missing for weeks or months before the crime."

"I doubt it."

"And the crime happened Sunday night?"

"Yes."

"Well," he said, "we have reports on four women who vanished between Saturday night and Sunday night, and are still missing. One of them was a woman of sixty-two. Think you might be interested in her?"

"I doubt it. Go ahead."

"Well, there was a woman of about thirty who walked out on her husband and two children. She would seem to fit most of the description of the woman found in the fire—except for one thing."

"What's that?"

"Her husband says that she wore false teeth, upper and lower," he said. He smiled up at me as if he were enjoying himself. "Then we have a woman of about twenty-five or six who disappeared Saturday night. She'd had polio when she was a child and her lower limbs were badly crippled. Lieutenant Arnold tells me that an examination of the victim's bones rules this one out."

"Go on," I said sourly.

"The fourth one was a woman of about thirty, but she was almost six inches shorter than the victim, according to the measurement of the bones from the fire."

"And that's all?"

"That's all. Of course, we get new reports every day and she may still come in. Some people don't report missing persons for a week or two. I've never been able to figure out why, but they don't. Or maybe she lived alone and nobody's missed her yet."

"I don't suppose any of Cantwell's girlfriends are missing or Lieutenant Arnold would have asked you specifically about them?"

"I don't think they are. In fact, I understand that all the known girlfriends are accounted for. I'm sure Lieutenant Arnold wouldn't mind me telling you this."

"Thanks for nothing," I said. "I'll maybe see you around."

"Always glad to be of help," he said with a broad grin as I turned away.

Downstairs, I looked at my watch and decided to knock off until it was time to go see the dentist. I drove around aimlessly, still followed by the same car, until I found a restaurant that looked appealing. I went in and had a couple of martinis and a leisurely lunch. When I left, I drove straight back downtown and went to the dentist's office. He and the doctor were both in, but I tried the dentist first.

The waiting room had a minimum of furniture and a few old magazines scattered around. There was no receptionist in sight. I sat down and waited. There was no sound of activity from the other room, and finally I went over and knocked on the door.

There was a moment of silence, then I heard a chair scrape on the floor, a filing cabinet drawer opened and closed, then there were footsteps across the floor. The door opened and a man looked out. He was probably no more than forty, although at first glance his face was gaunt enough to make him look older. He was in his shirtsleeves with tie loosened and collar open. There was a short stubble of beard on his face.

"Dr. Phillips?" I asked.

"Yes," he said. He stared at me curiously. "Are you looking for a dentist or are you merely another bill collector?"

"I think I'm looking for a dentist, but I'm not a bill collector. I'm afraid I'm not really a patient either. I'd like to ask you a few questions."

He sighed. "I should have known you weren't a patient. Well, come on in."

I stepped inside the office. It was furnished with the bare minimum needs of a dental office. There was a dental chair, a cabinet for dental tools and supplies, an extra chair, and a filing cabinet.

"There are only two places to sit," he said. "Take your choice."

"This'll be fine," I said, taking the dental chair. "It'll be the first time I've ever sat in one without something unpleasant happening to me. Is business as bad as you sound?"

"Business isn't bad," he said bitterly. "There just isn't any."

"What made it fall off?" I asked.

"There wasn't anything to fall off. I was a fool ever to open an office here. The only patients I've had were emergencies who merely wanted me to put in a temporary filling so they could manage until they reached their regular dentist. Well, my lease is up the end of this month and then I'll get out. I don't know why I'm telling you my troubles."

"Sometimes it's good to tell them to just anybody," I said easily. I took out a cigarette and lit it. I offered him one.

"No, thanks," he said. "I have only one bad habit. Since you are neither a patient nor a bill collector, I think I will indulge in it. Will you join me in a drink, Mr.—?"

"March. Milo March. I don't mind a drink now and then. Thanks."

He went to the filing cabinet, opened a drawer, and took out a bottle of bourbon. It was about two-thirds full. He took a glass from the same drawer, then got another one from the cabinet that held his instruments. He looked at me. "I don't have any ice."

"I'm not fussy," I told him. "I'll just have mine neat." He splashed whiskey into both glasses and handed me one. Then he went over and sat on the chair by the window. He took a quick gulp of the whiskey. "I won't be able to even afford this habit much longer," he said. "Well, Mr. March, what can I do for you?"

"Give me some information—if you have it," I said. I took a drink. It wasn't bad bourbon. "Something that happened two months ago."

"I've been here for a year and nothing has happened."

"Maybe it did and you didn't realize it. About two months ago there was a man who came to this building regularly. I don't know his last name, but his first name was Jimmy. If you saw him, however, you'd probably remember. He was from Skid Row around the corner and, I imagine, looked it and smelled it. I want to know if he came here to see you."

"There are a lot of offices in the building. Why pick on me for your questions?"

"I've talked to everyone else in the building," I said. This wasn't quite true, but he couldn't know that it wasn't. "Everyone else denied ever seeing him. That leaves you."

"Why would a man like that come to see me? Do I look like the type he'd visit?"

"You tell me if he did come to see you," I said, "and I think I can tell you why he came."

He looked at me with curiosity, the first sign of any reaction other than bitterness and resignation. "He said his name was James Smith. Now, why did he come to see me? And don't tell me that he came to have me look at his teeth."

I took a deep breath and let it out with a sigh. This was what I had wanted to hear and was what I'd felt certain about since I'd first gone through the building. It had to be the dentist he had come to at regular intervals.

"He came," I said slowly, "to have a lot of dental work done. But it was a very curious and unusual job."

"In what way?" he asked.

"Because you didn't tell the patient what should be done. He told you."

"I'll be damned," he said. He took another gulp of whiskey and looked up. "You're more or less right. There was another fellow with him the first time he came. They brought dental Xrays with them and said I was to make the bum's teeth match those in the Xrays. It was crazy, but they both insisted, and I needed the money. So I did it.

SEVEN

This, I told myself, could be the one break I needed. If I was right in my theory about the case, and this seemed to prove that I was, Dr. Phillips might be all I needed—once I caught up with Mr. Cantwell. The dentist's testimony might be enough to hold up payment of the insurance for some time, but it wouldn't be enough to ensure victory without turning up Richard Cantwell. But it was the first step—and a big one.

"Why are you interested in this?" he asked.

"Because I think those two men were involved in a fraud involving a lot of money. I work for the insurance company that was defrauded."

Then he looked alarmed. "I didn't know anything about fraud. Sure, I thought it was screwy as hell, but I wasn't involved in anything but doing my job."

"Sure," I said. "I believe you. I know how much money was involved and I don't think I'd find you here like this if you'd been a part of it. But I'm not so sure that a court would look at it the same way. You say you were just doing your job. Did you get your degree with the understanding that you were going to fill teeth that didn't need it and put inlays in perfectly healthy teeth just because, as you say, you needed the money?"

"What do you mean?" he asked nervously. He gulped the

rest of his whiskey and went over to pour another drink. This time he didn't offer me one.

"It's simple enough," I told him. "Whether you knew about it or not, whether you were to share in the proceeds or not, you were an accessory to the crime. If you cooperate with us, I think I can assure you that my company will be grateful and will be convinced that you were an innocent dupe. If you don't, they may feel quite differently about it and I can't guarantee what will happen."

"There are always threats, aren't there?" he said bitterly. "You said there was a lot of money involved. How much?"

"At the moment, almost a million and a half dollars. I think it was meant to be almost two million, but there was a slight slip-up."

"The sonofabitch," he said angrily.

"What's wrong? You say that you weren't part of the scheme and you were paid well enough for the work you did, weren't you?"

He laughed without humor. "You think so? I'll tell you about it, Mr. March. The two of them came in here one day two months ago. The one that was the bum, and the other man who was obviously wealthy and accustomed to having his way. They had nothing in common but the fact that they were together."

"Did they introduce themselves?"

"Oh, yes. The bum was James Smith. The other man introduced himself as Mr. Richards—a name I suspected of being as phony as that of Smith."

"It was. Go on."

"I suspect that the one who called himself Mr. Richards may have made inquiries about me, and already knew before he came in that I had very little practice. But he came and looked around and you could almost see him writing up an inventory of everything in my office and putting a price tag on it." He paused a minute, then plunged ahead. "I've been here for almost a year with nothing to do but sit around and wait for patients who never came. Finally, in desperation, I began to drink a little about six months ago. It has probably saved my sanity. But I think that your Mr. Richards knew that I had been drinking and this made him feel superior."

"Well, I think he has done a few things worse than drinking," I said. "What did he do?"

"He looked at me as if he knew how badly I needed money and he despised me for it. It was the same way that he looked at the bum. He told me that his 'friend' needed some extensive dental work that would take about two weeks to complete, working steadily. He explained that would include fillings, inlays, one false tooth, and a bridge. He wanted to know in round figures how much it would cost. I told him that I couldn't say exactly until I had examined the patient, but he interrupted to inform me that I didn't have to examine the patient; he had just told me what was required and all I had to do was give him a price—unless I didn't want the business."

From what I knew of Cantwell, this sounded exactly like him. "So you gave him a price?"

"Sure. I needed the money. I gave him a price. It wasn't high but it was one I thought would cover me. He came back with an offer which was about two-thirds of what I had said and told me to take it or leave it because he wouldn't pay me a cent more. He picked up his hat and was ready to leave—so I took it. I didn't have much choice. The sonofabitch."

"Then he told you what he wanted done?"

"Yes. He gave me an Xray and said I was to make the bum's mouth so that it would exactly match the mouth in the Xray. I asked the bum if that was what he wanted, too, and he said it was. So I did the work. I had to take Xrays every day to make sure that what I'd done the day before was right. When I'd finally finished, nobody could have told one set of Xrays from the other."

"And you were paid?"

"Yes." He poured himself another drink. "And you know what that bastard did? He gave me a fifty-dollar tip. A tip! Like I was a waiter or something."

"What did you do?"

"I took it. I told you I needed the money—still do. So I'd probably take a tip from anybody. I'd like to have thrown it in his face, but I didn't. I put it in my pocket and watched them walk out."

"Have you ever seen either one of them since then?"

"No."

"Those Xrays," I said. "Do you still have them?"

He shook his head. "That was part of the bargain. I had to turn all the Xrays over to him. He even went through my files to be sure that I'd given him all of them."

"Well, I thought that was too much to hope for. But you'd recognize both men if you were to see them again?"

"I certainly would. You bring them around and I'll identify them for you."

"I'd like to," I said, "but I'll have to find them first. Did you have an address for either of them?"

"Yes, for the bum. But I don't have any of the records on him. The other man took them as well as the Xrays."

"Can you remember the address?"

"I remember it. It was the Fitch Hotel on Fifth Street—a flophouse. Fifty cents a night for a bed. I walked by it once out of curiosity."

"Are you going to be here the rest of the day?"

"Sure. I don't have anyplace to go. And somebody might come in with a toothache."

"Okay," I said. "I'll see you soon."

He was staring dumbly at me as I left. I went downstairs and found the nearest liquor store. I bought three quarts of good bourbon and told the clerk to deliver them to the dentist. I checked the time. It was almost five o'clock in New York. I stopped in a drugstore and put in a call to Martin Raymond at Intercontinental. It took a few minutes for the call to go through, then he was on the phone.

"Was just wondering when I'd hear from you, Milo," he said. "How's it going, boy?"

"Pretty good, I think," I said. "I guess by now you know that the second body in the fire wasn't the wife?"

"Yes. I saw a report from the L.A. office. Good news. That takes us off the hook for at least five hundred thousand."

"Yeah, but you're on the hook for another five hundred thousand we hadn't counted in the total."

"What do you mean?"

"Cantwell embezzled slightly more than that from the

company. Although he was stealing from himself, it was still stealing and if we can't prove that he's still alive, I think you might have to pay it."

"You think he's still alive?" he asked. "You mean that it was a double in the fire?"

"I'm positive," I said. I told him about the dentist. "It's enough to convince me, but it won't be enough for a court. I don't think he can get away with it, although finding him may be a long job."

"That's good work, Milo. You stick to it and do the best you can. In the meantime you've found enough so that we can stall when the widow demands payment."

"I may need some more money."

"Anything, Milo, boy. Just see the manager in the Los Angeles office."

I decided I'd better quit while I was ahead. "All right, Martin, I'll let you know what happens."

"Keep in touch, boy. We're counting on you."

I hung up and walked over to Fifth Street. I soon saw the Fitch Hotel. It looked like a flophouse. I entered and was hit in the face by the combined odor of unwashed bodies and what was probably generous applications of Clorox.

There wasn't much in the lobby. There was a battered desk, a dog-eared entry book, and a pencil on it. There was a single chair back of the desk and, seated on it, a man who was half asleep. At first glance he looked more like a customer than a clerk.

He heard me approaching and partly succeeded in opening his eyes. "Just sign your name, put down your fifty cents, and take the second room on the right upstairs." Then he got a good look at me and his eyes opened all the way. "I guess you don't want a bed," he added sourly. "What's the beef this time?"

"No beef," I said.

"You're a cop, ain't you?"

"Not exactly," I told him. "I want some information. About a man who stayed here two months ago."

"Hell, they come and go here, and all of them look alike. I don't pay no attention to them."

"I think you might remember this one. He stayed here for at least two weeks. His name was Jimmy. He was fairly prosperous by the standards of Skid Row. But at the end of the two weeks I think he might have been even more prosperous and that he left. Does that ring any bells?"

"I ain't paid to remember who comes or leaves."

I pulled a ten-dollar bill from my pocket and put it on the desk. "Does this help your memory any?"

He picked up the bill and slipped it in his pocket. He gave me a toothless grin.

"Funny how a little thing will happen and suddenly you can remember clear as a bell. Yeah, I remember Jimmy. He'd been around for a long time, but usually he couldn't afford anything better than a twenty-five-cent bed and sometimes not that. I was surprised when he moved in here. But he came up with the fifty cents every day for two weeks. And when he left—that was the damnedest thing I ever seen here."

"What do you mean?"

"It was the kind of thing that you'd never forget when it happens down here in a flophouse. That last day he went out and came back with a lot of boxes. I thought maybe he had swiped some stuff somewhere. Then, in about two hours, he came down and I didn't recognize him. He was still half loaded, but he'd shaved and he was all dressed up in expensive clothes. He stopped and told me that he wouldn't be staying here after that day. Then you know what he did?"

"What?"

"Took out a roll of bills that would've choked a horse and gave me a tip of five bucks. I've been working in this joint for two years, and every minute I had to watch to see that nobody stole my pants off me. And this Jimmy comes down and tips me five bucks like he's been doing it all his life. Then he goes out and hails a taxi and goes off. A taxi!"

"Any idea where he went?"

"He didn't tell me. And I couldn't hear what he said to the cab driver."

"Did you notice what kind of taxi it was?"

He shrugged. "It was a taxi. That's all."

"I don't suppose the driver was one you recognized? One that works down here frequently?"

"No taxi works down here frequently. They merely pass through."

"And you haven't seen Jimmy since then?"

"No."

For a minute I'd been feeling elated, thinking that this was going to be as profitable an interview as the one with the dentist, but now the feeling was gone and I knew that it was a dead-end street. What I had learned fit in with everything I'd picked up in the last two days, but it didn't lead anywhere.

"Okay," I said. "Thanks for everything."

"Don't mention it," he said and flopped back in his chair. His eyes were already closed, then they suddenly popped open again before I had turned away. "Say, mister, where did Jimmy get all that money?"

"A fairy godfather," I said sourly.

"A fairy godfather?" He stared at me a second, then laughed, a high-pitch crackle. "A fairy godfather! That's a corker. I got to remember that one."

He was still laughing as I went out into the clean, fresh air of gasoline fumes and smog. I walked back to the Cadillac and drove uptown. I didn't have any idea what I was going to do next and it was only the middle of the afternoon. Suddenly, on an impulse, I swung over to Sunset Boulevard and kept going until I reached the hotel where Harry Manfred was staying. I drove into the parking lot, then entered the hotel. I went to the house phones and asked for Lillian Cassidy.

My hunch had been right. The operator merely asked me to wait a minute. She was soon back. "Miss Cassidy left word that she's at the pool."

I thanked the operator and went through the lobby to the pool. It wasn't hard to spot her. There were plenty of beautiful women around the pool, but only one with the combination of flaming red hair and arrogant breasts. She was wearing a bikini and the result was almost the same as when I'd seen her in my room. She was stretched out in a beach chair in front of the pool. I walked up behind her until I was near enough to touch her.

"Hello, Torchy," I said.

She turned to look at me. A slight narrowing of her eyes was the only sign of surprise. "Hello," she said. "How did you find me?"

"Called a friend in New York and asked him if he knew anybody named Torchy. He told me he did, and I figured you'd be staying at this hotel."

"Your friend a cop?"

"Yes."

"Then he must have told you that I don't have a record."

"He did. He seemed to think that you should have a record, but admitted that you didn't."

"You're pretty smart," she said. "I was told that you were, but I didn't think you were as good as you are. You were pretty tricky last night. I didn't think you could move that fast."

"I didn't. You nicked me on the shoulder."

"That wasn't what I was there for. I'm sorry."

"I've had a hangnail that hurt worse, so don't worry about it."

"The rest of it was a dirty trick," she said. "Pouring whiskey all over me and putting me in that car. Even the cab driver who brought me back here thought I was drunk, and was debating whether he should take me to the nearest police station or not."

"At least it kept you from making another try last night," I said.

"That it did. Now—what's this bit?"

"What bit?"

"Coming here to see me. You can't do anything to me for last night. You can't even prove I was there."

"I wasn't intending to try."

"Then why are you here?"

"First, to see how you are."

She rubbed her jaw and smiled. "A little sensitive, but otherwise all right. What's the other reason."

"I'm at loose ends for an hour or so and thought I'd offer to buy you a drink."

"I'll accept," she said promptly. "But I'll have to change clothes. Want to have the drink in my room or in the cocktail lounge?"

"In the cocktail lounge, honey. I don't have that much time. Besides, I don't want to make it too easy for … your friends."

She laughed. "It's not my job anymore. I fell on my face last night, so it was taken away from me. I'll meet you in the bar in fifteen minutes." She got up and walked away. It was the first time I'd ever seen her walk. It was a nice sight.

I went back into the hotel. I had fifteen minutes to kill, so I found a phone booth and called Pamela Cantwell. I made a date to pick her up again that night. Then I went into the bar and waited.

Torchy was prompt. It was just sixteen minutes when she showed up. Except for the first few seconds the night before, I couldn't honestly say that I'd had a good look at her. It's difficult to see very much when a gun is being pointed at you. Now I realized she really was a lovely woman; beautiful with a special sensuality in her face and in the movement of her body.

"Did you come around for our date—the one we talked about last night?" she asked as she joined me at the table.

"No," I said honestly. "I wanted to talk to you. Dates shouldn't be rushed."

"All right. What are we drinking?"

"I'm going to have a martini. What would you like?"

"The same."

The waiter came and I ordered two martinis. We talked nonsense until he came back with the drinks. When he was gone, I lifted my drink.

"To you, honey," I said. "And the next time you come to my room and take off your clothes, don't have a gun in your hand. It inhibits me."

"I won't. I told you that I don't have the job now."

I tasted my martini. It was excellent. "You work for Harry Manfred, don't you?" I asked casually.

"Your cop friend tell you that?"

"Yes. It's true, isn't it?"

"I know Harry Manfred," she said carefully. "I've done a few things for him. Little things, nothing important."

"What about last night?" I asked gently.

"You don't expect me to answer, do you?"

"No. Let's try another category. Last night, when you told me that you were called Torchy, I thought it was because of your hair. That's not true either. You're called Torchy because you're a professional match for Harry Manfred, aren't you?"

"This is a hell of a way to work up to a date," she said.

"I suppose it is. Torchy, you're the one who set the fire out at the Santa Monica beach Sunday night."

"And you're an insurance cop," she said. "Is that what you're trying to tell me? If so, why did you bother to even come here? You could have just stayed away and let it go at that. But I can take a hint." She stood up.

"Sit down," I told her. "It isn't any different from what it was last night."

"What does that mean?" she asked suspiciously.

"Last night you were out to frame me so that I couldn't continue working on the case I'm on. But that didn't stop you from talking about us getting together sometime in the future. Isn't that true?"

"So?"

"So I'm telling you that it still applies to us. You work for Harry Manfred and I think it was you who set that fire last Sunday night. If that's true, then I'm out to get you—but that shouldn't stop us from having drinks together or maybe even that date sometime." I beckoned to the waiter and ordered two more martinis.

"If what you say was true and you did catch me, I wouldn't be around for that date for a long time."

"That's true," I said cheerfully, "but that's what I call the risks of my profession. The same thing might be said of your profession."

"No wonder I liked you last night," she said slowly. "You're a real grade-A bastard, aren't you? What do you want from me?"

"Nothing special, honey. You're a good-looking broad, and I'm crazy about women." The waiter brought the drinks and I waited until he left. "Besides, you were frank with me last night and I'm returning the compliment."

"There has to be more to it than that."

I shook my head. "Not really. How could I be trying anything more? I don't even know how deeply you're involved. I know that somebody hired Harry Manfred to set fire to that house. He and his two strong-arm boys came out here to supervise the job and probably to make sure that they collect. There's a lot of money involved. I think that you did the actual torch work. If I'm right, that would complicate my wanting anything else out of you."

"What does that mean?"

"It's simple," I said. "Two people died in that fire. That makes the charges arson and murder in the first degree. I don't see how I could possibly talk any sort of deal with you under those circumstances, so you shouldn't be so suspicious of me."

She was staring at me intently. "You talk a lot and I can see you haven't finished yet, so go ahead."

I smiled at her over the top of my glass. "As I said, I wouldn't have any authority to talk any sort of deal with somebody guilty of first-degree murder. On the other hand, if you—and I'm just ad-libbing now—were to tell us everything we want to know, including who hired Manfred, the insurance company might take the view that you didn't really know that there were people in the house, and might throw their weight in favor of reducing the charge to second-degree murder or manslaughter. I don't know that they would, of course, but it is a possibility since they have a lot of money at stake. Anyway, it makes interesting speculation."

She threw her head back and laughed. "A gold-plated

bastard," she said, "but interesting. I hope that we can get around to that date. If I were guilty of what you believe, wouldn't I be a fool to take up an offer that isn't even an offer? It's a maybe. And if I were guilty, it wouldn't make any difference whether I was executed by the state for breaking one law or by someone else for breaking another one."

"I suppose so," I agreed. "I was just being as frank with you as you were with me last night. I was thinking out loud, as they say in certain circles. Now, honey, I have to run along. But I'll be around."

"I expect you will be," she said. "I'm going to stay here for a few minutes. I may have another drink to get over the shock of being turned down."

"You haven't been turned down, honey. There's always tomorrow—as you pointed out to me last night. See you later."

I went over and paid my check. Then I took the elevator up to the floor where Harry Manfred had his suite. I knocked on the door and waited. It was opened by the same man who had opened it the day before. The one called Eddie. He recognized me at once.

"Hey, boss," he called over his shoulder, "it's that insurance dick."

"Bring him in," the voice said.

"Inside, sucker," Eddie said.

"That's what I came for," I told him. I walked past him into the suite and on into the other room. Harry Manfred, dressed in an imported silk suit, was sitting in a big chair and reading a New York paper. His other boy, the one called Jim, was hunched over in front of the television set watching one of those games where the participants win prizes.

"Turn off the set, Jim," Manfred said without taking his gaze off me.

"I didn't find out if the broad wins the fur coat," Jim complained.

"Go buy her one," Manfred said shortly. "Turn it off." He waited until the set was off, then spoke to me. "I was expecting you, March. What took you so long?"

"What's that supposed to mean?" I asked.

"You arrived here at the hotel almost an hour ago. I figured you'd come right up."

"I get it," I said. "It was you who were having me followed today."

"You're a busy little man," he answered. "What do you think it's going to buy you?"

"I'll get something out of it."

He pointed a pudgy finger at me. "I don't like it, March. I've been talking to some of my friends in New York. I knew what you did in New Orleans, but I've been getting the big picture of you. I don't like it. You're getting in my hair."

"Is that a subtle way of calling me a louse?" I asked.

Eddie laughed. "Hey, that's a good one, boss."

"Shut up," Manfred said. "He made the joke, not me."

"I've been talking to my friends in New York, too, Manfred," I said. "I picked up a few interesting things. I knew all about you, but I found out that you have a girl working for you. She's called Torchy and she's a match. Last night she tried to put me in a frame and hang me on your wall. She's quite a girl, but I guess you know it didn't work out."

"I don't know nothing about any broads," he said. "I'm clean, March. So get off my back before something happens to you."

"I've heard that from others. I'm still around."

"You never heard it from Harry Manfred before."

"Besides," I went on, "I haven't been on your back. I've been on the back of the man who hired you."

There was a knock on the door. The three men exchanged glances and Eddie disappeared into the other room. A moment later he was back and Torchy was with him. She didn't even blink when she saw me there.

"What do you want?" Manfred demanded.

"It's okay," she said. "He knows that I work for you. He checked with the cops in New York. But I told him there's nothing moving now and this is just a vacation."

"How come you know what he knows?" Manfred asked.

"He told me. He picked me up at the pool about an hour ago and wanted me to have a drink with him. We had two in the bar downstairs. And you know what else he thinks? He thinks I set that fire that happened out at Santa Monica Sunday night. Ain't that a laugh?"

"Yeah, it's a laugh," Manfred said sourly. He looked at me. "So that's where you were?"

"Can you think of a better place?" I asked lightly. "Or better company? I felt I owed her a visit in return for her call on me last night."

"I've had enough of this," Manfred said tightly. "What the hell do you want, March?"

"I don't want anything. I'm doing fine. But I thought I'd give you—or any one of your group—a chance to get in a better position before it's too late."

He glared at me. "You got something to say, you say it."

"You," I said to Manfred, "were hired to set fire to that house on Santa Monica beach. Torchy here did the actual job, but you and your muscle boys came along to see that there were no slip-ups, and to collect the money. After all, your cut of eight hundred and fifty thousand dollars, or more, adds up to a lot of money. Naturally, you wanted to protect it. Right so far?"

"Keep talking," he said hoarsely.

"Since two people died in that, fire," I continued, "the charge is murder in the first degree. If nothing else, all of you are accessories before the fact—and the penalty is the same. I can't make any promises, you understand, but I think that if one of you were to tell us all you know, my company might use whatever influence it has to see that a lighter charge was made against that person. I thought I'd just let you know about it."

Harry Manfred said a short, ugly word. It was one that you don't hear in mixed company unless they all know each other very well.

To my left, I heard Eddie move impatiently. "Want me to take him, boss?"

"Don't be a jerk," Manfred snapped without taking his gaze from me. "We don't take nobody here. Besides, I'm clean."

"I think you've been using the wrong kind of soap," I said gently.

He shifted his gaze to Torchy. "Is that what he told you downstairs while you were drinking?"

"That's about it," she said. "I didn't know he was going to tell you the same thing, so I came up to tell you."

He looked at me again. "You got anything else to say, March?"

"That's all," I said. "If you know anything about the person who hired you, then you must know that I'm getting closer all the time. I just wanted to give one of you a chance to be on the winning team."

"Sure," he said. He bit the word off as if it were something unpleasant he'd started to eat. "I don't like you, March. Besides, you're dangerous. And my friends in New York tell me that you can't be bought. Is that so?"

"I don't know. I never have been bought. Maybe that means that I can't be bought or maybe it means nobody ever offered the right price."

"How much do you make as an insurance dick?"

"A hundred dollars a day and expenses."

"When you work," he said. "Okay. How'd you like to work permanently for me at two hundred dollars a day and expenses? Every day. Even if you go to Palm Springs for a vacation."

"Like tomorrow?" I asked.

"Anytime you want."

"I don't think it would work out," I said. "I wouldn't mind spending my coffee breaks with Torchy, but I'd also have to associate with you and your two gun boys, and you're just not my type. I guess I was never meant to get rich."

"Boss ... ," Eddie began.

"Shut up." Harry Manfred looked at me without emotion. "Get out, March. And don't come back. If you do, I'll let Eddie and Jim throw you out. They'd like that."

"You can say that again, boss," Eddie said eagerly.

"I'm legit, March," Manfred went on. "There ain't nobody can pin anything on me, not even the Feds. And don't think they ain't trying. But the books say I'm clean. And no insurance punk is going to get away with trying to pin something on me. I don't care how tough he is. So you get off my back and stay off, or you'd better take out some of your own insurance."

"Okay," I said cheerfully. "Now it's my turn. You're not clean. You've just been able to get away with it—until now. Some of your friends have tried to put me away and didn't get any farther than the nearest friendly jail or morgue. No fat hood in an imported suit is going to play footsie with me. I'm going to stay on your back until you have saddle sores. In the meantime, I didn't make my offer to you. I made it to some of the people with you who might decide they don't want to go down with you. But we don't run our specials every day, and time is getting short."

His face had gotten darker as I spoke. "Get out," he said when I'd finished. His voice was so hoarse I could barely understand him.

"I think you know where I'm staying," I said with a smile. I turned and walked out. No one said anything.

Downstairs, I got the Cadillac out of the parking lot and drove up Sunset Boulevard toward Santa Monica. It was still early, but I didn't have anything else lined up for the day. I felt that I'd done enough. I'd uncovered quite a bit through my visit to the dentist, and I'd stirred up Harry Manfred enough so that he'd almost have to do something unless he was innocent. And there was about as much chance of that as there was that I was the Queen of England.

I reached the hotel and put the car in the parking lot. I stopped off in the bar and had a drink. I picked up a paper and went to the bungalow.

I undressed and went into the bathroom. I shaved and took a hot shower. Then, with a towel wrapped around me, I went back to the bedroom. I picked up the phone and put through a call to Lieutenant Arnold at the L.A. police.

"This is Milo March," I said when he answered. "How are you?"

"Fine," he said carefully. "How are you?"

"Couldn't be better. How are things going on our case?"

"We're working," he said, "as we always do. I hear you've been around to Missing Persons to ask a few questions."

"I've been working, too," I admitted. "Have you dug up anything new on the case?"

"Nothing I'd care to give out for publication, but I think I can say that we're making progress."

"And expect to make an arrest any minute," I added. "What about Manfred?"

"We've checked him out. He had an alibi for the time the fire must have been set, but then we didn't expect to find that he set it himself."

"And his two boys?"

"They had alibis, too. We figured the match was someone who's staying away from Manfred. But we'll find him."

"Sure, you will," I said, smiling into the phone. "Tell me, did you find anything near the fire that might be tied onto the match when you finally get him?"

"Well, there's the method. Almost every professional has his own method and it's different from all the others. If he has a record, we may be able to pin it to him because of that."

"And if he doesn't, you're working in a vacuum even after you find him. No, I meant did you find anything personal that could be tied to him?"

He hesitated a minute and then decided to answer. "We're not sure. The two bodies were on the second floor. We found a ring on the ground floor. It was a woman's ring. It may have been dropped by the arsonist, or it may have belonged to the woman who was upstairs."

"What kind of ring? Any way of identifying it further?"

"A diamond. The stone is preserved, of course. The ring itself was badly melted, but we did manage to get something out of it. There were initials and a date inside the ring. We couldn't restore the date enough to read it, but the lab thinks the initials were L.C. So if we find a professional match with a wife or girlfriend with those initials, we'll have a tie-in to him. Or it may be a clue to the girl upstairs."

"Sounds like a good possibility, Lieutenant."

"I'm glad you think so," he said. "I've done my cooperating. How about you now?"

"I have a thought for you," I said. "Are you certain that the male body in the fire was that of Richard Cantwell?"

"The identification was positive. What are you driving at?"

I'd decided I was going to tell him the two things that he'd probably find out anyway. "The identification was made by Cantwell's personal dentist, right? Well, did you know that about two months ago somebody broke into the dentist's office and stole, among other things, the Xrays of Cantwell's teeth?"

He swore. "Where did you learn that?"

"From the dentist. I've got another little haymaker for you. During the past few months, Richard Cantwell dipped his fingers into the till of his company for more than a half million dollars. And last Friday, just two days before the fire, he cleaned out his personal bank account. That's a lot of green stuff, Lieutenant, for a man to carry around just for cigarette money. I'd like to know where the money is now and who's with it."

"So would I," he said fervently. "Maybe I was wrong about you, March. Thanks. I didn't know about either one of those things. And somebody is going to get chewed out because I didn't. Anything else?"

"That's all at the moment."

"Okay. Keep in touch." He sounded almost warm as he finished talking and hung up.

I had two more calls to make. I called the manager of the local office of Intercontinental. He came on at once.

"Glad you called," he said. "We checked out those three Japanese for you. They're above reproach. There's no evidence that they ever met Cantwell, although I suppose they have at some time, since he was in the business of importing Japanese products. But Cantwell apparently never went near the foundation. Also, there's no way that any one of the three men could ever get directly to the money of the foundation. The only person who could is the Japanese girl who runs it. You want us to check her out, too?"

"No, I'll handle that myself."

"I had a call from the New York office telling me to let you draw any expense money you wanted."

"I may be dropping around for it," I said. "Thanks for the assist. I'll call or see you in the next day or two."

Next I called the hotel in Beverly Hills. When the operator answered, I asked for Lillian Cassidy.

"Hello," she said after a minute.

"Are you alone?" I asked.

"Yes. Who's this?"

"Milo March."

"You've got more guts than brains," she said. "Are you tired of living or something?"

"No. I just don't have the patience for the usual methods. I find that things work a little faster if I do some pushing."

"Okay, honey, but you don't push a bottle of nitro. And you didn't do me any favor with that offer. I'm getting the fish eye all the time now. I tried to tell him that you didn't mean it, but he thinks you did."

"I did," I said. "In fact, I called because I think you ought to give a little special attention to it."

"You think I'm crazy?"

"No. That's why I'm suggesting it. Torchy, did you lose a diamond ring recently?"

I could hear her gasp over the phone. "How did you know? Did you find it?"

"No, the police did. They found it in the ashes of the fire in Santa Monica."

There was a pause before she said anything. "They can't prove it was mine. It must've melted in the fire."

"Some, but not enough. The police lab managed to bring out the initials L.C. on the inside of the ring. I think they might do a pretty good job of tying it to you."

"Did you tell them it belonged to me?"

"Not yet."

"Why?" she asked. "I don't get it."

"I'm giving you a chance to do something to help yourself, but you don't have much time."

"I still want to know why. You don't know me that well. I tried to pin a frame on you last night. You're sure that I set that fire, which makes me the enemy. So why are you trying to do me a favor—not that I'm sure it is one?"

"I'll tell you, honey. I told you that I want to get the person who hired Harry Manfred. That's true. But I want to get Manfred, too. And I will, too—one way or another."

"I can't figure you," she said slowly. "You act like you were an army or something, but you're not even working closely with the cops. You're just one guy and you're trying to buck a guy who's fought armies all his life and won. How the hell do you expect to get anywhere?"

"I work differently," I said. "How about it, Torchy?"

"I'd be crazy to do anything you want me to," she said, and her voice sounded shaky. "You ought to know that. How long do you think I'd last, supposing that I know anything, if I was to talk?"

"I don't think you have much choice," I said gently. "The police will sooner or later connect that ring with you. They'll make a good enough case. Sure, it'll be mostly circumstantial, but a lot of people have gone to the gas chamber on circumstantial evidence."

"They'd never get to me if you weren't around to tell them."

"They still would. They'll find out about you and they'll get all the information the New York police have just as I did. But I'll be around and that's the other half of it."

"Meaning what?"

"I told you that I believe in pushing and I'm going to keep pushing. If you think Manfred is giving you the fish eye now, wait a few days. He's going to do more and more thinking about you. He'll start with the fact that you fell down on the job last night even though you had a gun on me, and he'll work on up through the offer he knows I made. The more he thinks, the more he'll believe."

"Like I said," she said dully, "you're a gold-plated bastard. Just leave me alone, will you?"

"Think it over, honey," I said and hung up.

I thought it had been a pretty good day. I set the clock, made sure that the doors and windows were locked, stretched out, and went to sleep.

The alarm woke me up in plenty of time for my date. I got dressed and then made my preparations. I'd pushed enough that I knew. I'd better be ready the rest of the time until the case was over. I buckled on my shoulder holster, made sure my .38 was loaded, and put it in the holster.

I decided I'd better have a little extra insurance. I had an old four-barreled derringer that I'd had a gunsmith bring up to date. The gun was small enough to fit into the palm of my hand, but it would fire four .32 bullets and had often come in handy. I got it out of my suitcase and loaded it. I had two holsters for it. One that could be worn on my arm and one that strapped around my leg below the knee. I used the latter and fixed the gun in position. It wasn't a very romantic way to go on a date but it made me feel a little better.

I pulled up in front of the house in Beverly Hills at the time I'd said I would be there. Driving down, I'd checked all the way and I hadn't been followed. I went up to the front door. The maid let me in and showed me into the same room where I'd waited the night before.

Pamela Cantwell showed up almost immediately. This time she was wearing a red dress that made her look like a goddess of flame. She came over and kissed me lightly on the cheek.

"I'd just been hoping that you would call when you did this afternoon," she said. "You know, it had been so long since I'd really had anything that could be called a date that I'd forgotten what it was like."

"What was it like?" I asked.

"It was wonderful," she said. "A martini before we go?"

"Sure."

As though she'd heard us, the maid came in with the pitcher and the martini glasses. She put them on the table and left. Pamela poured the drinks and handed me mine.

"To you," she said, "for making me feel like a woman again. What are we doing tonight?"

"Dinner first. Then we're going pub crawling. But before we leave, I want something from you."

"What?"

"A photograph of your husband. Do you have one?"

"He had dozens of them around all the time. They're still in his room. Why do you want it?"

"I need it for some of the work I'm doing."

"You still have that foolish idea that Richard may still be alive, don't you?"

"Yes."

"Will that delay me in getting the insurance money?" she asked anxiously.

"It ought to speed up the decision of the insurance company," I said evasively.

"I'll get it right now." She got up and left the room. She was gone about five minutes and then was back with a five-by-seven picture. "Will this do, Milo?"

I took the picture and looked at it. This was the first time I'd seen a photograph of him, but he looked exactly as I had imagined he would. It was a heavy face, with pronounced jowls, yet obviously without fat. It was, I supposed, a handsome face, but there was something in the expression that indicated much of the character back of it. This was a man who would not hesitate when there was something he wanted. Looking at the picture, you could imagine him as a very successful businessman—which he had been—or an equally successful pirate—which is what I thought he was at the moment.

"This will be fine," I said, slipping the photograph into my pocket.

We finished our drinks and left. This time we tried a restaurant on one of the side streets in Beverly Hills. It was filled with movie stars, which seemed to please Pamela, and it also had good food, which pleased me. We took our time over dinner and when we'd finished it was a good pub-crawling hour. I paid the check and we took off.

Our first club was on the Strip. We got a table and ordered drinks. There was a very smooth orchestra playing and we danced two or three times. Then I excused myself and went to the men's room. On my way back I found the headwaiter. I slipped him a twenty-dollar bill.

"I'd like some information," I told him.

Headwaiters have a highly developed tactile sense. I've long been convinced that they can tell the denomination of a bill just by feeling it. This one was no exception. He didn't look at the bill, so far as I could see, but his expression changed as he slipped it into his pocket. "Yes, sir?" he asked.

"Do you know this man?" I asked, taking the photograph from my pocket. He glanced at it.

"Yes, sir. That's Mr. Cantwell. He came here quite often. I was very sorry to read about his death in the papers."

"He came here often? How often?"

"Once or twice a week as a rule."

"With different women?"

"You're not a newspaperman, are you?" he asked.

"No. I'm with the insurance company that carried his insurance."

"Well, I wouldn't want to be quoted on it, sir. I know that Mr. Cantwell was married and there's no point distressing his widow more than is necessary."

"I agree."

"The truth of the matter is that Mr. Cantwell was very fond of women and he always had good taste. Usually he'd be in with the same woman for two or three months and then there'd be a new one. All of them young and all of them beautiful."

"What about recently?"

"Four or five months ago there was a new one and she lasted longer than usual. As a matter of fact, they were in here for a while last Saturday night."

"What did she look like?"

"A little like the lady you're with, sir. The same size and build and coloring, only quite a bit younger."

"What was her name?"

"I don't know, sir," he said. "I don't believe that I ever knew the names of any of the young ladies he brought here."

That was as far as I got. I went back to Pamela and after another drink we moved on. We stayed in each club for one or two drinks and then hopped to another one. But the story was the same in each. Cantwell had been a more or less regular patron of most of them. He'd been in with a variety of girls, but the last few months it had been the same girl. While the description pretty much tallied with the first one I'd gotten, nobody knew who she was.

About midnight we ended up in another club back on the Strip. We were just in time for the floor show, which consisted mostly of beautiful girls. In between numbers, I excused myself and slipped away. I found the headwaiter and again brought out my photograph. I had already parted with the usual twenty-dollar bill.

"That's Mr. Cantwell," he said.

"Was he a regular customer?" I asked.

He smiled. "He was here almost every night unless he was out of town on business or up in Las Vegas for a few days."

That was the first I'd heard about Las Vegas. "Did he go to Las Vegas often?" I asked.

"Fairly often. I believe he enjoyed the games, and I'm sure he could afford them."

"I understand that he had quite a string of girls."

He smiled. "He was fond of beautiful girls. And he could also afford them."

"What about recently? Say, the last four or five months. Did he bring in a lot of different girls, or was it always the same one?"

"It was the same one in the last few months."

"When was the last time they were in here?"

"Sunday night. The night he was killed."

"Who was the girl?" I asked, expecting the usual answer.

He looked at me, and from the expression in his eyes I knew that at last I was going to hit pay dirt. "Are you with the police?" he asked.

I shook my head. "I'm with the company that carried his insurance."

"I thought it was something like that," he said with a smile. "The police don't usually part with any money when they want to ask questions. Do you have any identification?"

I took out my wallet and showed him my Intercontinental card, my license as a private investigator, and my gun permits. It seemed to satisfy him.

"That is Mrs. Cantwell with you, isn't it?" he asked.

"Yes," I said in surprise. "Did he bring her here, too?"

"Only once. I believe it was about a year ago. I thought I recognized her."

"Let's get back to the girl Cantwell had been seeing."

He sighed heavily. "Come into the office for a moment, Mr. March. I'd rather talk in there than here." He motioned to a man on the floor to take his place and then led the way to a small office. He indicated a chair beside the desk.

"Have a drink, Mr. March? On the house."

I nodded and he brought out a bottle of V.O. and a couple of glasses from a small cabinet beside the desk. He poured the two drinks and pushed one over to me. I took it and waited, anticipating that he intended telling me all that he knew.

"It will all come out soon anyway," he said. "Mr. Cantwell owned this club."

He was certainly full of little surprises. "That's news," I said. "Neither his wife nor his accountant knows anything about it."

"I don't think that anyone knew about it except two or three of us here and Mr. Cantwell's lawyer."

"How long had he owned it?"

"About a year. This is related, Mr. March, to the question you asked. The girl was Betty Stellar. A year ago she was working here as one of the featured showgirls. Mr. Cantwell made a big play for her, but in the beginning she wouldn't have anything to do with him. My impression of Mr. Cantwell was that he always got what he went after—one way or another."

"I think that's probably true," I said. "How did he do it in the case of this girl?"

"I'm not sure," he said slowly. "One of the first things he did when she wouldn't see him was to buy this club. He paid cash for it."

"Who'd he buy it from?"

"Me. I was operating on a narrow margin, but I was making money, so I refused to sell when he first offered. He finally offered so much money, plus a good salary to operate the place for him, that I couldn't refuse. I sold it to him. I don't know how he used this against Betty. I don't think it would have worked to threaten to fire her or anything like that. But within about seven months she quit her job, and after that she was with him almost every time he came in."

"I think I can understand it," I said. "Success has its own attraction. The man who is certain that he can get what he's going after already has an advantage."

"I suppose so. I'll be perfectly frank with you, Mr. March. I didn't like Cantwell. I didn't like working for him and I didn't like having him around. Betty Stellar was one of the nicest girls here, though. She was no tramp. You can ask anyone who worked here. I hated to see her get mixed up with him, but it was none of my business, so I kept out of it. And she seemed to be happier recently. Especially so on Sunday night."

"Any idea why?"

"I don't know, although I can make a guess. Knowing her, I'd bet that she thought Cantwell was going to leave his wife and marry her."

"There's no indication that he was planning anything like that," I said.

He smiled crookedly. "I didn't say that I thought he was going to. I said that she probably thought he was." He was silent for a second, then looked directly at me. "You think it was her in the fire with him, don't you?"

"I think it was her in the fire," I said. "I'm just trying to put all the pieces together."

"Why?" he asked. "If someone deliberately killed the two of them or the fire was an accident, it doesn't change the insurance picture, does it?"

"We like to know how these things happen. And if the fire was deliberately set, which makes it murder, we're interested in who set it. That could change our picture."

He stared at me. "You mean his wife … ? You suspect her?"

"I suspect everybody—until I know. Anyway, there was a second beneficiary in the event that Mrs. Cantwell died. And it was believed at first that the woman in the fire was Mrs. Cantwell."

He was looking at me curiously and I decided I'd better stop his flow of questions. "I'd better get back to Mrs. Cantwell," I said. "Do you have an address for Betty Stellar?"

"When she first came to work here, she was living with her parents out in the Valley. Sherman Oaks, I think. Later she moved into the city, but I don't know where." He opened a small file and started looking through the cards. He pulled one out. "Here it is. It was Sherman Oaks." He found a blank card and copied down the address. He pushed it across to me.

"Thank you," I said. "You've been very helpful and I appreciate it." I started for the door and he had to go along with me.

"Let me know what happens," he said. "I'm interested. If I can be of any more help, I'll be glad to do anything I can."

"I will," I told him. "I'll probably be around."

"Thanks … I guess I'll just keep on running the place on receipts until Mrs. Cantwell decides what she's going to do with it."

"Maybe she'll sell it back to you," I said. "Well, thanks again." I left him and went back to the table.

"You were gone a long time," Pamela said. "I'd started to think that you had walked out on me."

"Was that because you wanted me to?"

"You know better than that," she said. "I told you that you have made me feel like a woman again. It's been a long time since I felt like one."

"I'm glad," I told her, reaching over to touch her hand.

"But tonight," she went on, "I'm really only protective coloring, aren't I?"

"What do you mean?"

"You've left the table at each place we visited. And as soon as you returned, you were ready to go on to the next place. So you've really been working tonight, haven't you?"

"We'll stay right here until you're ready to go home," I told her.

"You didn't answer my question, Milo."

"I've been working," I admitted, "but that doesn't mean

that you were protective coloring. I could have gone to all of these places by myself. I wanted you to come along and that's why I invited you."

"Did Richard go to all of the clubs we were at tonight?"

"Yes. He even brought you to this one. About a year ago, I think."

"I remember. I recognized it the minute we came in. Since it was the only time he took me out in over a year, I remembered it. He was entertaining some business associates and they had their wives along. So we all came here. Did—did he come here often?"

"Yes."

"With other women?"

"Yes."

"And that was what you were checking up on tonight?"

"No. I've been trying to get some lead to who the girl was who was found in the fire."

"Any luck?"

"Just now. That's why I was gone so long. I think that it must have been the girl he was seeing most recently. All of the clubs reported seeing him around with the same girl in recent months, but at the other places they didn't know who she was. Here, they did."

"Who was she?"

"Her name was Betty Stellar. She used to be a showgirl here."

"I'm sorry for her," she said gently. "I mean that she had to die like that. Was she in love with Richard?"

"I think she imagined that she was."

"I guess I was once in love with Richard. Now it's difficult to imagine that any woman could be in love with him. I'm sorry if that seems harsh, but that's the way it is. What are you going to do with what you learned?"

"Check it out and then turn the information over to the police."

"If she was in the fire," she said, "that would indicate that it was really Richard who was there, and it upsets your theory, doesn't it?"

"Maybe. We'll see."

We had a couple more drinks and talked about other things. Finally she said she wanted to go home. I called the waiter and asked for the check. He went away but was soon back, empty-handed.

"Mr. Velli says that you don't get a check," he reported. I handed him a good-sized tip and we left.

"What was that all about?" she asked as we got into the car.

"Oh, I forgot to tell you something," I said. "It would seem that you now own that nightclub. So I guess that's the reason."

She looked at me in astonishment. "You mean … ?"

"He owned it. For the last year. I understand that it's making money, too."

"How long have you known this?"

"I just learned it tonight."

She leaned back against the seat and laughed. "Of all the things to inherit!

Maybe I'll go work in the line myself."

"You'd be the prettiest one there," I said, and was rewarded by having her lean over and kiss me on the cheek.

I drove straight back to her house. She wanted me to come in, but I begged off. I wanted to be up early the next morning and I had a notion I'd need all of my senses to get through the day. I took her to the door and kissed her good night. She leaned against me and suddenly her body stiffened.

"Is that a gun?" she asked.

I admitted it was.

"Why?" she asked. "What are you going to do?"

"Go back to the hotel and go to sleep," I said truthfully. "I sometimes wear a gun for the same reason a woman wears a girdle. It doesn't make me more romantic, but it does give me a sense of security."

"Milo, please be careful," she said. "You—maybe you don't know what you're up against."

"I know, honey," I told her. "I'll call you tomorrow."

I watched her enter the house and then I went back to the car. I drove to Santa Monica and put the car in the hotel parking lot. I walked across to my bungalow, making sure that I didn't use a route where I could be surprised. I unlocked my door and reached in to snap on the light. The room looked as it had when I left. Just to be sure, I drew my gun before I stepped inside.

But I'd made a mistake. I knew it as soon as I was in the room. I didn't see or hear anything. I simply sensed the movement as someone came out from behind the door. When I tried to whirl around, it was too late. Something landed with a dull thud just above my ear and there was a flashing of lights inside my head. I could feel my knees bending as I sagged toward the floor.

Then something pulled a black cover over my head, and that was all I knew.

EIGHT

There was too damn much noise. Someone was hammering away inside my head with a pile driver. There was a radio or television set going somewhere, only the music sounded as if it were coming from a boiler factory. Nearer, somebody was drumming on wood in time to the music, and I could feel every blow he struck. I was about to complain about the noise when my memory began to come back. Somebody had been waiting behind the door in my room and had slugged me over the head.

I kept my eyes shut until I remembered all of it up to the point of blacking out. Whoever it was must have taken me someplace. I could feel that I was sitting in a chair, so I wasn't still in transit. I wasn't alone. There was a television or radio program on. That was about all I could tell with my eyes shut. Slowly I opened them partway.

It was a large, comfortable room that looked as if it might have been part of a hunting lodge. The furniture had that look. There was a big stone fireplace without a fire. There was a well-stocked bar along one wall. Beyond it, I could see another room with a pool table in it. I looked around at the rest of the room. There was a big color TV set with a musical on the screen. And there were two men. One of them was Jim Warren, the other Eddie Hale—Manfred's gunmen.

Jim had his coat off, and the shoulder holster and gun were prominent. He was the one who was drumming in time to the music. Eddie had his gun in his lap with his hand on it. He was looking straight at me.

"Well," he said, "the big, tough guy is finally awake. Turn the TV down, Jim."

"Hell," Jim said. "That's all anybody ever says to me. 'Turn the TV down.' 'Turn the TV off.' There's a good crime picture coming on the late late show."* He got up and lowered the volume on the set.

"Were going to do our own movie," Eddie said, "so forget about it. How do you feel now, tough guy?"

"Lousy," I said. I struggled to sit up and the pain shot through my head. "Did you have to hit me so hard?"

"Why not? That shouldn't have been too hard for a guy who's supposed to be tough. Besides, it won't make any difference in an hour or so."

"That's nice," I said. I pretended to straighten my clothes and explored my right leg. Then I felt a little better because my little gun was still there. They hadn't found it. I made a more obvious move of touching my shoulder holster.

"We pulled your teeth, junior," Eddie said. He was enjoying himself. "I've got the gun. I may keep it to remember you by."

"I'll give you something better," I said. I rubbed my aching head. "Do you mind if I have a drink? I need it."

"Help yourself," he said, waving the gun. "But don't get any ideas."

---

* In the 1960s there was a syndicated movie show on TV called *The Late Show.* After 11:30 p.m. there was also a *Late, Late Show.*

"Don't have room for ideas right now," I said. I stood up and waited until the dizziness passed. Then I walked over to the bar. I found a glass and filled it half full from the first bottle I grabbed. It was brandy. I took a drink and made my way back to the chair. I was feeling a little better by the time I got there.

"Where's the rest of the mob?" I asked. "Manfred and Torchy."

"You'll see them soon enough."

"You mean you're going to keep me alive that long?"

"It won't be so long," he said.

"Do you have to talk?" demanded Jim. "The comedian is on now and I can't hear what he's saying."

Eddie told him what he could do with the comedian, the television show, and the set.

"Where are we?" I asked.

"You ever hear of Topanga Canyon?"

I nodded.

"Well, that's where you are. Harry owns the place. We brought you up here to keep you on ice until everything is ready."

"Until what's ready?"

He grinned broadly. "You know, things have changed in the business. There was a time we'd have gunned you down in your hotel room and left it at that. Now we play it like it was legit. Harry's got a friend out here who owns a boat. In about an hour or so it's going to be anchored off the shore about five miles from here. Jim and me will get a phone call and then we drive down there and we all go in a small boat out to the big one. Harry will be there waiting for us. We take you out about twelve or fifteen miles, put a hole in you with your own gun, and dump you and the gun overboard. Then we go home to sleep like any other honest citizens."

"Sounds exciting," I said. I was busy casing the room and wondering how I was going to make my play.

"If you get any bright ideas before we get the call," Eddie said, "we can always put the bullet in you here and still take you out to sea. It's up to you, sport."

I looked and sure enough it was my own gun that Eddie was holding in his lap.

"I'm getting tired of being held up with my own gun," I said wearily. "How are you going to explain what happened to me?"

"We ain't going to explain it. While we're doing this, Torchy's going around to your room and pack up all your stuff and move it out. We'll burn it. So maybe you just skipped out on your hotel bill and ran off with some broad. Or maybe you got paid off and went somewhere to spend your money."

"Like Cantwell?" I asked.

"Something like that, yeah. Only they won't get the chance to look at your teeth—unless they do a lot of swimming."

"Sounds like you worked real hard on this one. Well, in the meantime things have to go on. Where's the bathroom in this joint?"

"In the next room. But I go with you."

I sat back down. "You're not my type. Thanks, I'll just hold everything in for the time. When did you say you're going to get that phone call?"

"Maybe an hour, maybe two. They have to come up from

San Diego, so it'll be whenever they get here."

I crossed my legs and put my left hand on my ankle. If I was careful I might be able to work my hand up inside the trouser leg until I reached the gun. I'd still have to get it out and that was going to be cutting it pretty fine with Eddie sitting there, his gun ready.

"Didn't you give any thought to what I said this afternoon?" I asked.

Eddie grinned. "Sure. This is the answer."

"It's not very smart," I said. "The police have one clue that will lead them right to your door. And they have other leads that will take them to the person who hired you."

"The cops," he said with contempt. "They couldn't even catch a cold. All kinds of cops have been trying to get us for years and they ain't even got to first base."

I'd reached the gun and started slowly working it out of its holster. "I'm sort of a cop, so why are you bothering with me?"

"You cause too much trouble, running around trying to get somebody to squeal.

Besides, nobody is calling Harry Manfred a fat hood and getting away with it."

"The boys back in New York won't like it."

"They'll put up with it."

"Okay," I said. I'd worked the gun down to my ankle. I concealed it in the palm of my hand and brought it up to my lap. I hid it there, finished my drink, and lit a cigarette. I pretended to shake out the match, but kept is lighted as I dropped my hand over the side of the chair that was away from him. It wasn't a very good idea, but it was the best that

I could think of. I held the match up against the chair until I could feel the chair material catching fire. It was just in time, for the match burned my finger. I dropped it and hoped that the chair would continue to burn.

I transferred my cigarette to my left hand and got my right hand on the derringer and waited. "You know," I said, "you really might get off easy if you talked. This is a big case and my company would lean over backward to help anyone who helped them."

"You're wasting your breath, tough guy," Eddie said. He kept his gaze steadily on me. "Hey, Jim, do you hear the tough guy? He's trying to talk his way out of the big swim we have planned for him. Maybe he ain't so tough after all."

"Don't bother me," Jim said. "The crime movie's starting. Both of you talk too much."

"I'm getting a little tired of the conversation myself, Jim," I said. I leaned back in the chair and tried to give the picture of relaxation. My left elbow was over the edge of the chair aim and it was getting so warm I knew the chair must still be burning.

A couple of minutes passed in silence except for the sound of the television. My elbow was getting uncomfortably warm and I had to move it. I almost held my breath as I waited. If it worked, it would give me something like a tenth of a second. It might be enough—and it might not. I certainly couldn't afford to waste any time.

Eddie's face wrinkled up and I could see he was sniffing. "It smells like something was burning," he said.

"Probably my cigarette," I said. "Want me to put it out?"

"No," he said shortly. He was staring at me suspiciously. "You trying to pull something, sucker?"

"How can I pull anything with you watching me?" I countered. I could hear the faint sound of burning to my left, and knew the flame should soon be in sight. I tensed myself.

Then it happened. I couldn't see it, but the flame must have worked up above the chair. Eddie's eyes flicked to my left, and the gun swiveled with them. I lifted the derringer.

I'd been right about the time. He caught the slight movement and turned back to me. I didn't have any time to be fancy. I had the derringer lined up on him and I pulled the trigger. His shirt front jumped slightly as the bullet hit. His gun went off, but he was already slumping over and the bullet went wild.

Then I learned something about Jim. Maybe he was wrapped up in television, but that didn't keep him from moving fast when it was necessary. Even as I turned toward him, he'd left his chair in a long dive to the floor, his right hand snaking the gun out of his holster before he landed. He snapped a shot at me before I could even line up the derringer. He was stretched out on the floor, propped up on one elbow, steadying the gun for his second shot. I had intended to try to wing him and take him in, but there was no time. I centered the derringer and pulled the trigger. He jerked once and fell back, his gun cracking against the floor.

I went over and put out the fire. Then I sat down and shook for a while. That had been a close one. Too close.

Finally I got up and went over to look at both of them. They were dead. I went to the door and looked out. The house sat up on a hill and there wasn't another house in sight. There was a car parked in front of the house. I closed the door and turned back to the room. The television was still blaring away, but I didn't go near it. I walked over to Eddie and picked up my gun and put it in the holster. I dropped the derringer in my coat pocket. Then I went through Eddie's pockets until I found what I thought were the car keys.

I walked over to the bar and poured myself a drink. My head still hurt and I felt a little dizzy. I took the drink down in one gulp. Then I remembered I didn't have a bottle back in the hotel room. I took a bottle of V.O. and a bottle of rye from Harry Manfred's bar and walked out to the car. The keys were the right ones. I started the car and drove down to the road. I turned left and headed back to Santa Monica.

I parked the car two blocks away from the hotel and walked the rest of the way. As I neared my bungalow, I saw there were lights on behind the drawn curtains. I didn't know whether they'd been left on by Eddie and Jim, or if it meant that Torchy was there packing my things.

When I reached the door I stopped and set the two bottles down. I pulled my gun from the holster and tried the door-knob. It was locked. I got out my key, inserted it gently, and turned it slowly. The door unlocked without a sound. I put the key away and opened the door as silently as I could. As soon as it started to swing open, I gave it a strong push and stepped inside.

Torchy was across the room bent over my suitcase. She heard the door bang against the wall and whirled around. Then she saw me and her face went white.

"Going somewhere, honey?" I asked.

She opened her mouth but no sound came out. She closed it, swallowed, and tried again. "You—you're not supposed to be here," she said.

"I know. But I've never really liked swimming in the ocean."

"Eddie and Jim?"

"I'm afraid they had a slight accident. Slight, but fatal. Sit down, honey. You don't look as if you feel well. You carrying a gun?"

She nodded and sank down on the couch. "In my bag." I walked over to her bag on the coffee table. I opened it with one hand and reached inside. I pulled out a .32 with a two-inch barrel. I broke it open and ejected the shells. Then I put it back. I put away my own gun and went to the door to get the two bottles. I closed the door and walked across to where she was sitting. I put the bottles down.

"Pour yourself a drink. You look as if you need it. Pour one for me while you're at it."

She got up and went for the glasses. She poured a generous amount of whiskey in each glass. She half emptied hers in one swallow. Some of the color returned to her face. I got my own drink and sat in a chair across the room from her.

"What happened?" she asked.

"Everything went the way it was supposed to, except that I refused to cooperate all the way. I don't have much of a life, but I've grown rather fond of it."

"I don't understand. Eddie and Jim were two of the best guns in the business."

"They goofed, honey. They found one gun on me, but they didn't look too closely for a second one. You can't afford many mistakes like that."

"What are you going to do now? Turn me over to the police?"

"For breaking and entering? Don't be silly. If I ever get you, Torchy, it's going to be for the jackpot. Now, it's been a long day. I think you'd better run along and let me get some sleep."

"You mean it?"

"Sure. But you might give some more thought to what I said to you this afternoon. The circle is getting smaller all the time."

She finished her drink and got up. She picked up her handbag and walked to the door. There she stopped and looked back at me. "Milo," she said.

"Go home and think about it, honey," I said. "Good night."

She turned and left the room. I went over and made sure that the door was locked. I didn't think anyone would be back that night, but I took a chair and propped it under the doorknob as added insurance. I undressed and went to bed. I was tired enough to fall asleep the minute I hit the sheets.

I awakened about nine the next morning. I hadn't had enough sleep, but it would have to do. I was going to be busy. This was Friday. I'd arrived in Los Angeles Wednesday morning and I was getting impatient. I called room service and told them to send around bacon and eggs, toast, and coffee. I went into the bathroom and looked at my head in the mirror. I still had a lump and it was sore, but it was better than it had been when I'd come in last night. I took a quick shower and went back to the couch. I poured myself a drink and waited.

The waiter arrived with my breakfast and I ate it without fooling around. I picked up the phone and called Lieutenant Arnold.

"Good morning," he said. "More information for us?"

"In a way," I said. "Did you know that Harry Manfred owned a house out in Topanga Canyon?"

"Yeah, I know about it. I don't think he uses it much. Why?"

"Is it in your jurisdiction?"

"I guess so. Part of the canyon is in our territory and part is in the sheriff's. We usually work together when there's anything out there. Why?"

"Call up the sheriff and take a run out. You'll find two of Manfred's gunmen there. They're dead."

"Who killed them?"

"I did. They picked me up here last night and took me out there. They were going to kill me and take me out to be dumped in the Pacific. It was self-defense."

"And no witnesses," he said dryly. "What did you shoot them with?"

"A derringer that shoots .32 bullets."

"Got a permit for it?" he asked casually.

"Yes."

"City or County?"

"I have a permit that's good in the whole damned state for it and for another gun," I snapped. "What the hell are you trying to get tough about?"

"I suppose it was justifiable homicide, but we just don't

like anyone going around shooting people—even if they are hoods. Anyway, you'll have to come down and make a statement and stick around until we have a coroner's inquest."

"I know all that. I'll make a statement."

"When?"

"Later. I'm going to be busy this morning. I'll get around to it sometime later on."

"I could have you picked up."

"You try it," I said grimly. "My company's got enough power even out here to see that the whole thing gets aired. People will think that it's funny you let two New York gangsters hang around all this time without arresting them, and then arrest an honest citizen who kills them defending himself."

"All right," he sighed, "but just don't put off coming in too long. Why did they pick you up?"

"I guess Manfred thought I was getting too close to him."

"Maybe," he grunted. "Well, thanks, March, for calling me. I'll be seeing you later." He put a little emphasis on the last sentence.

"As soon as I can make it," I said and hung up. I glanced at my watch. It was almost ten o'clock. Time to get moving. But I wanted to make a couple of other calls first. For one thing, I wanted to push Harry Manfred a little more. I had a good idea about that. I picked up the phone and put in a call to a barbershop in a big hotel in New York. It would be almost one o'clock there, and there was a certain man who went to that barbershop every day between twelve-thirty and one. He was well known and had been called everything from the Prime Minister to the President of the Syndicate. I didn't know what his title was, but I knew he was about as important as they came in Manfred's circle.

Somebody answered with the name of the barbershop.

"Is the Big Boy there?" I asked.

There was a moment's pause. "Who is calling?" the man asked cautiously.

"Just tell him the call is from L.A.," I said.

There was silence for a couple of minutes and then a different voice came on. This one was hoarse and sounded tired. "Yes?" he asked. I recognized the voice. I didn't know him, but I'd heard him on television when they broadcast the crime hearings.

"You don't know me," I said, "although you may have heard of me. My name is Milo March. I'm an insurance investigator. A couple of years ago I helped put away a business associate of yours in New Orleans."

He was silent for so long that I thought he'd put down the phone and gone away. "I've heard of you," he said then. "What do you want?"

"Another business associate of yours is here in L.A. He came about a week ago and he's still here. Do you know who I mean or should I mention names?"

"I think I know who you mean."

"I thought you might be interested in him," I said. "He came here to do one of his usual jobs. He loused it up slightly. The police haven't caught up with it yet, but they will. They have something that will point right to him. I know about it. I've been on to a few other things, too, and he hit the panic button."

"What do you mean?"

"Last night he tried to kill me. The old-fashioned kind of thing. It's bad for your business."

"What happened?"

"He sent two guns. They were careless. I killed them. It'll be in all the afternoon papers and you can read about it. It won't be hard for the papers to find out who they worked for. And that'll be bad for your business, too."

"Who were the two?" he asked.

"Eddie Hale and Jim Warren."

"I know them. They're good men."

"Were," I said. "It's going to stir things up. I thought you'd like to know."

"Why?"

"Why what?"

"Why did you bother to phone? It must be going your way."

"It is," I said, "but I don't like your friend who's out here. I'll do anything I can to push him nearer to the brink. If you know what he's doing, you may even help me."

He chuckled, but there was no warmth in it. "I almost like you," he said. "You've got a lot of nerve. But didn't it occur to you that I might help my friend?"

"I don't think so," I said. "Everything I've ever heard about you tells me that you're a practical businessman—even though your business isn't exactly recognized by the Better Business Bureau. What your friend is doing now is bad for business. It might be even worse if he gets his way with me—because even if he does, I'll take a few people with me. I like company. And my company is Intercontinental Insurance, one of the largest in the world. They'll scream like a stuck pig. And when they scream, there are a lot of institutions in America that start trembling."

"I think I see your point," he said slowly. "I'm not sure that I should, but I'll thank you for your call. I'll think about it."

"It's getting close. I don't think your friend is going to make it this time."

"Good-bye," he said with finality. There was a click as he hung up. I smiled to myself and lit a cigarette. Then I called the desk clerk and told him I wanted the phone number of the airline that provided service between Los Angeles and Las Vegas. He gave it to me and I put in a call to them.

When they answered, I asked the reservation clerk if she knew the name of Richard Cantwell. She did. She told me that he had often traveled on their planes to Las Vegas, and she'd been very sorry to learn of his death.

"Had he made any new reservations around the time of his death?" I asked.

"No. Not for himself."

"What does that mean?"

"Well, he did phone in on Saturday and asked us to make a reservation for friends of his on a flight Wednesday morning. In the name of Mr. and Mrs. Richards."

"That's very interesting," I said. "Did Mr. Richards pick up his reservation?"

"No, he didn't. We held the ticket until Tuesday night and then canceled. I guess Mr. Richards decided not to go when he learned of his friend's death, and just forgot to call us."

"I imagine Mr. Richards was very touched," I said. "What time can I get a flight to Las Vegas this afternoon?"

"There's one leaving at two o'clock."

"Okay. Make a reservation in the name of Milo March, like in January, February, March. I'll pick it up at the airport."

"Yes, sir."

I hung up and went in to shave. Then I got dressed. I was just about to leave when the phone rang. I picked it up and said hello.

"Mr. March?" It was a man's voice and its tone was agitated.

"Yes."

"This is Mr. Patman. You know, the accountant at the Cantwell offices?"

"Hello, Mr. Patman," I said. "How did you get my number? I don't remember giving it to you."

"You didn't. I called the insurance company and told them it was imperative I get in touch with you. They gave me the number. I hope you don't mind?"

"Not at all. Is there something wrong?"

"I've just learned the most shocking thing. Actually it's two things, but I'm sure that they are related. I thought I should tell you."

"I appreciate it," I said. "What's happened?"

"Well, I had a call this morning from an official at the Universal Commercial Bank. We use them for certain of our overseas transactions and have an account there. They called about our notes. There is no record here in the office of any money owed them. But they say that a year ago Mr. Cantwell borrowed six hundred thousand dollars from them. He told them that he wanted it put in the domestic account, and so they gave him a check made out to the company instead of merely transferring the money to our account. There is no record of that six hundred thousand dollars ever being deposited in the other account."

"But the check was cashed?"

"Oh, yes."

"Did you ask them to check the endorsement?"

"Yes. It was endorsed by Mr. Cantwell. Then there was a second endorsement indicating that the check was cashed by the Chihuahua Hotel Corporation in Las Vegas, Nevada."

"That's very interesting."

"But that isn't all, Mr. March," he said. "I've been working very hard all week to get everything in shape for Mrs. Cantwell. Yesterday I thought I'd run across something, and this morning I started double-checking it. Our inventory doesn't agree with the books. I'm pretty certain that in a six-month period just prior to a year ago, Mr. Cantwell embezzled another five hundred thousand dollars from the business and covered it with fake vouchers indicating it was an inventory. Do you realize, Mr. March, that this shows that Mr. Cantwell stole more than one and a half million dollars from this company?"

"I had already added it up," I said dryly.

"What in the world could he do with that much money in a year and a half?"

"I imagine he found something to do with it. What's this going to do to the company? Throw it into bankruptcy?"

"I don't think so. We're doing considerable business and I'm sure the bank will give us a little time. We will have to pull in our belts a bit, but we should be able to get back on an even keel within a year or so. It is fortunate that we do have insurance against embezzlement."

"I'm not sure that Intercontinental will feel that it's so fortunate. Anything else, Mr. Patman?"

"Not at the moment, no. I'm still trying to check out everything."

"Good man. Incidentally, I told the police a little about Mr. Cantwell's activities and I imagine they'll be around to see you sometime today. I'll be in touch with you soon." I hung up and left.

I drove down to Hollywood and hit the Freeway to the San Fernando Valley. It was a fairly short drive to Sherman Oaks. When I reached there, I stopped at the first gas station for directions. Five minutes later I was knocking on the door of a small, neat house.

The door was opened by a dark-haired woman who was probably in her middle forties.

"Mrs. Stellar?" I asked.

"Yes."

"I'm interested in getting in touch with your daughter. I thought perhaps you could help me."

"Won't you come in?" she asked. I followed her into the house. She led me into the living room and asked me to sit down. "What is this about?" she asked.

"My name is Milo March," I said. "I work for an insurance company." I showed her my identification from Intercontinental and waited until she had looked at it. "It has to do with some insurance matters with the Copacasa nightclub in Hollywood. I understand that your daughter worked there, and I thought she might be able to give me some information."

"I'm sure she will if she can," she said. "Betty's a good girl and always does what is right. I'm afraid, however, I can't tell you exactly where to find her at the moment. I know that she's in Las Vegas but I'm not sure where she's staying."

"She doesn't live at home?"

"She did up until about six months ago. But she hated driving back and forth, especially late at night, and she took an apartment in the city."

"Where is it?"

"Cherokee. Twelve hundred. But she's not there just now."

"When did you last speak to her?"

"She called me last Sunday. She'd been out of work for a couple of months, since the club let her go, and she called to tell me that she had gotten a job in a hotel in Las Vegas and she would call me as soon as she got a place to live. She hasn't called me yet—which is not like her."

"When you do hear from her," I said, "I wonder if you'd call me and let me know where she is? I'm staying at the Pacific-Melton in Santa Monica."

"Of course, Mr. March. I'm sure she'll call today or tomorrow. As I said, it's not like her to go this long without calling."

I thanked Mrs. Stellar and left. I drove back into Hollywood and headed downtown. I parked near Fifth Street and stopped by the dentist's office. I didn't expect to find him there, but to my surprise he was.

"Ah, Mr. March," he said when he saw me. "That was most thoughtful of you yesterday. I want you to know that I appreciate it." He had obviously already been working on the gift.

"It was nothing," I said. "There may be more like it."

"You know, I was thinking, Mr. March. Insurance companies must have a use for dentists, just as they do for doctors. If your company really feels that I have been of use, perhaps they might have a position for me."

"I'll find out," I told him. I pulled the photograph from my pocket. "In the meantime, I want you to take a look at this."

He took the picture and looked at it. "That's him. That's the man who brought the bum to me. His picture was in the papers, too. That's Cantwell, isn't it? I finally read the papers today, first time this week. He's the one you want?"

"I'll tell you another time," I said, taking the picture back. "Tell me, Dr. Phillips, could you tell the difference between your own work and that of another dentist?"

"Of course. Any dentist could."

"Even if, say, the fillings were otherwise identical?"

"Yes. But I don't understand."

"Suppose that all of you had to go on were a man's teeth. And suppose there was a question of finding out whether the teeth belonged to the man you worked on or to the man whose Xrays you copied. Would you be able to tell which man the teeth belonged to?"

"Probably not, if I didn't know the situation. But knowing it and knowing what I was looking for, I certainly could. Each dentist has his own way of working and can spot it if he's looking for it. Does this mean Cantwell isn't dead?"

"Somebody's dead," I said.

"I understand," he said. "Will you join me in a drink?"

"Not this time, Doctor. But I'll see you again soon and we'll have a drink together."

I left and walked around the corner to the bar where I'd met Hank. He wasn't there. I ordered a drink and put a bill on the bar.

"Hank been around?" I asked the bartender when he brought my change.

"Not since he was here with you yesterday."

"What time does he come in?"

"Well, he don't come every day. Hank's a floater."

"How's that?"

"He floats around. I guess he gets tired of staying in one place. He's always been like that."

"How long have you known him?"

"I guess Hank showed up on Skid Row about five years ago. He was around for a while and then he vanished. He wasn't around until a few months ago. Since then he's been coming in some days and not others."

"Where had he been?"

"I don't know. He said something once about San Diego and Frisco. I suppose one Skid Row and one flophouse are no better than the ones in other places. Some of the boys around here think that Hank's got folks somewhere and that they maybe send him some money so he won't come home."

"Well, that's one way of living. How's he doing with the money I left here for him?"

"He's been working on it, but I guess he's got about two bucks left."

"Did you know Jimmy, too?"

"The same way I know them all. He was around."

"When he hit it rich, too?"

"Around here, hitting it rich only means having a few bucks. He bought some drinks, but that was all. Maybe he hit it rich and maybe he didn't."

"I hear he hit it richer than that. I hear that when he left, he was all dressed up and left in a taxi."

The bartender shrugged. "Maybe."

"He's never been back, has he?"

"No."

"Any idea where he went?"

"No."

"Did you know anything about him? Like where he came from or anything like that?"

"Mister," the bartender said, "down here, you don't know anything about anybody except what they drink."

"I'd like to find out where Jimmy went," I said. "Do you think anyone down here might have an idea?"

"Who knows?"

"I'll make you an offer," I said. "If you'll spread the word that I'll give fifty dollars to anyone who can tell me where Jimmy went when he left here, I'll also give you fifty dollars when I get the information."

"That's a lot of money," he said. "How do I know you're good for it?"

I pulled my money out and put two fifty-dollar bills on the bar. "Give me a receipt for these and I'll let you hold them until we find out what's going to happen." He scratched his head, looking doubtfully at the bills. Then he went and got a piece of paper and a stubby pencil. He wrote out a receipt and gave it to me. I stuffed it in my pocket and he tucked the bills under the cash tray in the register.

"I don't know," he said. "There may not be anybody who knows anything."

"We'll see," I said. "I'll drop in tomorrow." I finished my drink and left.

I had already talked to Patman, so I didn't bother stopping at the Cantwell Company. I headed back uptown, stopping off when I reached the Intercontinental offices. I went in and saw the manager.

"I was told to ask you if I wanted more expense money," I said. "So I'm asking."

"Certainly," he said. "How much did you want?"

"A thousand dollars will do," I said.

He looked startled, but he left and returned in a few minutes with a thousand dollars in fifties and hundreds. I signed for the money and stuffed it in my pocket.

"That's a lot of money," he said nervously. "I've never been authorized to do anything like this before."

"That's not a lot of money. Just wait until you see what the company has to pay out if I don't crack this case. And I need the money. I'm on my way to Las Vegas, and I understand they've raised the price of martinis up there."

He was still trying to think of something to say when I walked out. I got in the car and drove straight back to my hotel in Santa Monica.

I didn't know whether the Las Vegas trip would take long or not, so I packed a few things in a bag to take with me. I was reaching for the phone when it rang. I picked it up and said hello.

"March?" The voice sounded familiar, but I couldn't place it.

"Yes."

"This is Harry Manfred. I want to see you. Now." There was a click as he hung up.

I looked at my watch. I would have time to stop and see him before making the plane. Maybe one more little push would make him crack. I picked up the phone again and put in a call to Pamela Cantwell.

"Hi," she said when she came on. "You're getting me into bad habits."

"What does that mean?"

"I was accustomed to being lonely. Now you've got me waiting for the phone to ring. It's a bad habit."

"Not as long as the phone rings."

"I suppose so," she said. "Will I see you tonight?"

"I don't know," I said. "I'm just leaving for Las Vegas. I'm not sure whether I'll get back tonight or not. I'll call you when I do."

"All right." She hesitated and then went on. "Do you know a man named Harry Manfred?"

"I know him. Why?"

"There was a news broadcast on the radio a few minutes ago. It said that two gunmen believed to work for a Harry Manfred were shot to death in Topanga Canyon last night. It said they were killed by a New York insurance investigator. Was that what you left to do last night?"

"I didn't know it at the time, but that was what I left to do last night. I have to catch a plane now, honey. I'll call you when I get back."

"All right," she said dully.

I took my suitcase out to the car and drove to Beverly Hills. I parked by the hotel and went up to the tenth floor. I knocked on the door.

"Come in," he called.

I opened the door and stepped inside. Harry Manfred was sitting in a chair. There was a gun in his pudgy hand.

"Come on in, March," he said grimly. "You killed two of my best men last night. I'm not taking any chances with you."

NINE

Closing the door behind me, I walked on into the room. I took a chair across from him and, moving slowly, pulled out a cigarette and lit it. I smiled at him.

"You won't shoot me," I said. "You're too big a man to do your own dirty work anymore. Besides, the hotel probably wouldn't let you stay here again."

"I could claim self-defense."

"You?" I laughed. "With your record, do you think anybody would believe you?"

"All right," he said. "I didn't ask you here to shoot you. I'm holding the gun just in case you get any ideas. And don't think Harry Manfred's gone soft just because I can hire people to work for me. I can shoot just as well as in the days when I was working for the Brooklyn mob. If you don't think so, try me."

"I don't want to shoot you. I want to see you go to court. Did you have a nice boat trip up from San Diego last night?"

He swore under his breath. "What the hell happened? Eddie and Jim were two of the best men I ever had."

"They were careless," I said. "And they made the mistake that you hoods always make. They figured that any kind of a cop was too stupid ever to get the best of them. But I'm sorry I had to kill them. I'd rather have seen them get the gas chamber."

"All right," he said. "I've got some more boys on their way out. They'll be here this afternoon. What kind of a sonofabitch are you, March?"

"The usual kind. What's bothering you, Manfred? You hear the clock ticking in the background?"

He swore again. "You made a call to New York City this morning."

"Sure. What about it?"

"I don't get it. You called a guy who shouldn't even talk to you. He not only talked to you, but he called me later and wanted to know what the hell I was doing. How do you rate with him?"

"I don't rate with him," I said. "If he thought it safe, he'd have me killed the way he'd step on a cockroach. But he's smarter than you are. He knows it's not safe to kill me unless he has a foolproof method. And he knows when somebody gets careless, I usually nail him. He remembers the Painter."

"I remember the Painter, too. He was a right guy. But I figured he maybe just made a little mistake."

"That's all he did, Manfred. He made a little mistake. You've made a couple of little mistakes yourself."

"What do you mean?"

"You'll hear about them from the D.A. when the time comes. You know, I was kidding yesterday when I talked about a deal with anyone who would turn state's evidence, but don't make any mistake about this. I don't need a stool pigeon. I'm going to nail your hide, Manfred. Maybe not for the big score. You've got a lot of money and good lawyers, and maybe you can beat the rap for murder, but I'll put you away for enough years so that I don't think you'll live long enough to get out."

His face was dark with blood and there was a slight tremor in the hand that held the gun.

"Pull the trigger," I told him, "and even the money and the lawyers won't keep you out of the gas chamber."

He took a deep breath and relaxed slightly. "So maybe I made a mistake about you, March. Yesterday I offered you a job at two hundred dollars a day. So now I admit that wasn't enough for a man like you. Suppose I offer you a cut?"

"A cut of what?"

"I'm collecting more than a half million on a business deal that recently went through. Suppose I split it with you?"

"Who's paying you the money?"

He shook his head. "I never tell the names of clients even to people who work for me. Anyway, it's got nothing to do with you getting three hundred grand. In cash."

"That's a lot of money," I admitted. "What do you expect in return?"

"Nothing, except that you go off somewhere and spend it. I'll level with you, March. You're bugging me. Without you, the cops wouldn't get nowhere. And I got the word from New York today not to knock you off. That's the only reason I'm making you the offer."

"Your generosity overwhelms me," I said dryly.

"But don't make any mistakes," he said. "If you turn it down, I don't give a damn what word I get from New York. My other boys will be here, and I'm not going to let a lousy insurance dick put the arm on me."

"I don't think you should call me lousy," I said seriously, "when I'm worth three hundred thousand."

"Then you'll take it?"

"When would I get it?"

"As soon as I collect."

"When is that?"

"When the insurance company pays off."

"That could be a long wait, and I'm a heavy spender. Where do you have to go to collect the money?"

"That's my worry. I'll get it. Well, March?"

"It's a nice offer," I said. "About the nicest I've ever had. But I don't know. I like booze and broads. If I had three hundred thousand dollars I'd probably ruin my health in no time. And just at a time when the President is calling on all of us to become physically fit. No, I think I'd better turn it down."

"That's your answer?" he asked angrily.

"That's it."

"All right, March. That's your last chance. My boys will be here this afternoon."

"Give them my regards. Now I have to go catch a plane. But I'll be back. I'll see you in court, Manfred." I turned my back on him and his gun and walked out.

Downstairs I stopped long enough to get a letterhead and envelope and write a short note. I wrote: "Honey, the time is getting short. Pretty soon I won't need you. And neither will Harry. Milo."

I addressed the envelope to Lillian Cassidy and left it with the desk clerk. I went out and drove to the airport. I parked the car and locked it, then went in to pick up my ticket and board the plane.

The flight to Las Vegas is a short one. When we landed, there were limousines from most of the hotels, but I ignored them. I took a taxi and told the driver to take me to the Chihuahua Hotel.

The Chihuahua's one of those giant palace hotel–gambling house setups that Las Vegas has become famous for. It stands not far from the Sands and dozens of other similar places. I went in and told the clerk that I didn't have a reservation, but I wanted a room anyway. He signed me in and had a bellhop take me up to a corner room that was worth about twice what I was being charged. They expected to make up the difference on the tables.

I went downstairs to the bar and had a couple of martinis. I left a good-sized tip and went into the gambling rooms. There weren't too many players at that hour in the afternoon, but there were a few people getting rid of their money. I lost a couple of bucks on a slot machine and finally went into the main room. I bought some chips and looked around. I threw away forty dollars on roulette, then drifted over to the dice table. I picked up the dice and put fifty dollars on the table. I threw a seven.

I made four passes and there was eight hundred dollars on the table. I picked up the chips and gave the dice back. The house man shrugged and watched me as I went over to cash in.

"Is the manager around?" I asked the cashier when I had my money.

"Don't know," he said. "That's his office over there. Try, if you like."

I went across to the door that he indicated. There was a sign on it that said Thomas Ricci, Manager. I knocked on the door.

"Come in," a voice said.

I opened the door and stepped into the office. The man at the desk was probably in his middle thirties. He was slim and darkly good-looking. He wore a dinner jacket even though it was late afternoon. He looked a little like a gangster who had gotten some polish and gone legitimate—which was probably a good description of Nevada gambling.

"Mr. Ricci?" I asked.

"Yes. What's the trouble?"

"No trouble. I'd like to ask you a few questions."

His face smoothed out, devoid of expression, which told more about his background than anything else. He looked me over more carefully. "Cop?" he asked.

"Some people call me a cop. Cops don't. I'm an insurance investigator for Intercontinental Insurance."

"Something wrong with our policy?" he demanded.

"You're insured with Intercontinental?" I asked.

' "Of course. Isn't that why you're here?"

"No. There's nothing wrong with your policy so far as I know. But since you're a policyholder with us, maybe you'll feel like giving us a little cooperation."

"Like how?"

"Know a man named Richard Cantwell from Los Angeles?"

"The guy who died in a fire down there last weekend?"

"That's the one."

"You got anything to prove who you are?" he asked.

I brought out my identification and showed it to him. He examined it carefully and handed it back to me. He looked me over again. "You're carrying a rod," he said.

"Yeah," I said.

"All right," he said. "I knew Cantwell."

"How long?"

"He'd been coming here for about a year and a half."

"How often?"

"Usually once a week. Sometimes he'd skip a week. Usually he stayed only a day or two."

"Alone?"

He smiled. "No. He always had a broad with him. All of them were dishes."

"How much did he lose?" I asked.

"How did you know he lost?"

"It figures. How much?"

He hesitated but then decided he had nothing to lose. "Over the year and a half, he probably lost six or seven hundred thousand here. I don't know how much he lost in other places."

"He played in the other clubs?"

"Sure. A lot of our tenants do occasionally. They think it'll change their luck. Or they get up a party to go to another hotel to see the floor show and they play awhile. The people from the other hotels do the same thing here. So it levels out."

"Did he always pay or did he stick you for some of it?"

"He paid," he said flatly.

"Cash?"

"Cash. We don't often take checks here—although we did take one large one from Mr. Cantwell once. It was a bank check."

"Cantwell was a heavy loser?"

"Pretty heavy. I guess he could afford it."

"Do you know if he made a reservation to come up this week?"

"No. I would have been told if he had."

"Did he come without a reservation?"

For the first time he showed some expression in his face. "What're you talking about? The guy was killed in a fire Sunday night."

"All we've got from the fire," I said, "is a set of teeth and some bones. And we have a guy who lost maybe close to a million dollars in a year and a half. Maybe a guy like that would think that his insurance money looked pretty good."

He smiled. "I get it. If he did that, I wish he'd come here with the loot. But we haven't seen him."

"Could he have checked into the hotel under another name and be lying low?"

"I doubt it. You couldn't keep him away from the tables that long. Ask the desk clerk. Everybody here knew him. He'd have trouble coming in without being recognized."

"Okay," I said. "Thanks for the help."

"On the house. You staying long?"

"I don't know."

"About that gun," he said. "We don't like to have them brought into the game rooms. It makes everybody nervous."

"I'll remember it," I said. "I guess I'll have to give up

gambling. You wouldn't want me to go out without my shoes and catch pneumonia."

He smiled thinly and glanced down at the newspaper on his desk. It was a Los Angeles paper. "Insurance investigator, huh?" he said. "I was just reading this story when you came in. You the one who gunned down those two boys in L.A. last night?"

"I'm the one," I admitted. "They didn't like the work I'm doing, but they got careless."

"You must be good," he said. "Those boys had pretty good reps. The paper says they worked for Harry Manfred. He mixed up in this Cantwell thing?"

"Up to his eyebrows."

He had a cautious look on his face again. "You got it pinned on him?"

"Not yet, but I will," I said. I smiled down at him. "Manfred's getting careless. Maybe he's getting too fat. I called a barbershop in New York this morning. Since then I think Manfred has been told to stay in line."

"Oh?" he said casually. "Who'd you talk to in New York?"

"The Big Boy."

"You know him?"

"Not personally. But I have known some of his business associates and he knows my name."

"You get around, don't you? Maybe you should have told me all this first."

"It doesn't make any difference," I told him. "I'm not after any publicity, so there won't be anything released about how much Cantwell lost and where he lost it."

"Maybe I should remember you anyway."

"Only if you decide to set this place on fire to collect the insurance," I told him with a smile. "Thanks, again." I went out and found the desk clerk. I showed him the picture of Cantwell. I thought I'd test the statement that everyone knew him well.

"That's Mr. Cantwell," the man said. "He was one of our best customers. I was sorry to hear of his death."

"I can imagine," I said. "Did he have a reservation for this week?"

"No."

"Did he come this week without a reservation?"

He looked shocked. "The man died Sunday."

"Maybe, but that doesn't answer my question. Is he here now?"

"Of course not."

"Could he be here under another name without you knowing it?"

"No. He was well known to all of our employees. He was a good tipper. His presence would be reported to me at once."

"Thanks," I said. He was staring thoughtfully after me as I left.

I tried the picture out on some of the others. The bartender, the elevator men, and several bellhops. All of them recognized it and all of them reacted the same way when I wanted to know if he was staying there. By the time I'd finished, half of the hotel was convinced that I was some kind of nut.

I left the hotel and started making the rounds of the other places. In almost every gambling place the photograph of

Cantwell was recognized, and everyone said they hadn't seen him in more than a week. But I did learn that he had lost somewhere near three hundred thousand dollars in other spots. That meant he'd lost about a million dollars in a year and a half. No wonder he'd started dipping into the till when the losses started. It also explained the borrowing he'd done from the bank. The early embezzlement and the loan just about covered what he'd lost. And it could explain why he'd decided to make one last grab in a try for the insurance money.

I went back to the Chihuahua and checked on planes to L.A. There was one leaving in about two hours. I had my dinner in the hotel, then went in to the tables. I won another couple of hundred on the dice tables. I saw Ricci wandering around but he paid no attention to me. I went upstairs and got my bag and checked out. I took a taxi to the airport.

It was still early when I reached L.A., but I decided not to call Pamela Cantwell. I felt like being alone. The case was making me itchy. I had a feeling of being so close to having it wrapped up that I could almost taste the victory—yet there were too many pieces just beyond my grasp. I didn't know what was bothering me. I had made a lot of progress in the few days I'd been there, but I was bothered by the open spaces that I hadn't been able to fill. Where had Jimmy the bum spent his time until he was needed? Where was Cantwell? How was he going to collect the money? Was his wife in it with him, or was he certain that he could handle her later? Why had he let his girlfriend be killed in the fire, too?

I drove down to Hollywood and did some pub crawling by myself. It didn't help. Finally, I went back to Santa Monica.

This time, I covered all the angles when I entered my room, but there was nobody there. I tried watching television, but it only bored me. Then I had a few drinks from one of Harry Manfred's bottles and went to sleep.

It was eight o'clock when I got up. I ordered my usual breakfast. I thought about the case while I ate. I had done about all the pushing of Manfred that I could. I had to dig up more about the other end of the conspiracy.

The phone rang. I picked it up and answered. "March," he said, "this is Lieutenant Arnold. I thought you were coming down to see us yesterday."

"I was, but I was busy until late last evening. I'll be down right away."

"I think that's an excellent idea."

"Will you be there?"

"I'll be here."

"Then I'll see you," I said cheerfully. I hung up and finished my coffee. Then I got dressed and left.

The Lieutenant was waiting when I got there. A police stenographer was with him. I dictated a full statement of what had happened the night before last, and the stenographer went off to transcribe it. I turned and looked at the Lieutenant.

"Does that make you feel better?" I asked.

"Not much. I still don't like citizens going around shooting each other."

"I would've called and asked your permission, but there wasn't enough time to look up your home number. When's the coroner's inquest?"

"Next week. You'll be there?"

"Do I have a choice?"

"No."

"Then I'll be there. How's the case going?"

"All right. The information you gave me checked out. I'll have to say that for you."

"I think I have some more," I said. "I think I know who the girl in the fire was."

"Who?"

"Betty Stellar. She used to be a dancer at the Copacasa club. Her parents live out in Sherman Oaks, but she had an apartment at twelve hundred Cherokee for the past six months. The parents don't know that she's missing. She talked to them last Sunday and said she was going to Las Vegas to work, and that she'd get in touch with them as soon as she had a place to stay. They haven't heard from her yet."

"Maybe she did go there to get a job."

"I don't think so. She told her parents that she lost her job at the Copacasa a few months ago. She didn't lose it. She quit when she became Cantwell's girl. And they wouldn't have fired her for that. Cantwell owned the club."

"You've been a busy little fellow, haven't you?" he said. "How do you figure it? Why would Cantwell knock her off if your theory is right?"

"I don't know. Maybe he believed that 'he travels fastest who travels alone.' How are you making out with Manfred?"

"We're watching him. I think the best we can hope for him is to keep watching until he goes to collect money from someone. How are you making out with him?"

"Fine. He offered me three hundred thousand dollars yesterday."

"Why?"

"To leave him alone."

"How do you rate that? I haven't seen you come up with enough to be worth that much. Or are you holding out on me?"

"I've been pushing Manfred. That's why he sent the two guns after me. He can't take much pushing."

He grunted. "How'd you find out about the girl?"

"Footwork. I just went around to clubs until I found out who Cantwell's latest girl was. That was all there was to it."

"Well, maybe it's the girl and maybe it isn't. We'll follow it up. Thanks."

"You're welcome. How about you telling me something now?"

"Nothing to tell you," he grunted. "But we're working."

The police stenographer came back with the transcript of my statement. I read it carefully to make sure that nobody had pulled a fast one on me, then signed all the copies. I exchanged a few more pleasantries with the Lieutenant and left. One thing was certain. He was never going to be very crazy about insurance investigators.

I didn't have anything special in mind to do. All I could do was keep digging in the same ground I'd already fenced in. So I drove downtown to Fifth Street and parked. I went over to the bar. There were two men drinking wine at the far end of the bar. Neither of them was Hank. I went in and sat on the nearest end of the bar. The bartender came over.

"V.O. on the rocks," I said. "Any luck?"

He poured the drink and took my money. "Not yet. I've been spreading the word, but nothing's come up yet."

"Well, keep at it. Hank been around?"

"Not since day before yesterday."

I finished my drink and walked around the corner to the Cantwell offices. The girl told me to go right into Mr. Patman's office. He was bent over his desk, which was piled high with papers and books. He looked up as I came in.

"Oh, hello, Mr. March."

"How's it going?"

He shook his head wearily. "Sometimes I feel I'll never get through all of these papers. Everything is so tangled."

"Find anything new?"

"Not since yesterday. I'm trying to go through and get a clear picture of the shape the business is in. Mrs. Cantwell may want to know. Do you suppose she'll keep the business?"

"I don't know. If it's successful, I would imagine she might."

"Maybe Henry Kray will come back to the business," he said. "That is, if she knows where to find him. I wouldn't mind working for him."

"Why would she bring him back?"

"Well, Mrs. Cantwell and Mr. Kray were always friendly. Oh, I don't mean there was anything wrong in the relationship. It was nothing like that. But they had much in common—books and music and things of the sort. When she came to the office—she used to come down often in those days—they would talk. I don't think Mr. Cantwell liked it. But then he didn't want anyone being friendly with Mr. Kray."

"Then maybe he will come back to work," I said. "Well, I just thought I'd drop in to see if you'd fished up any more startling news."

"No," he said. "I'll tell you, Mr. March, this is enough to make a man give up. There are things here that I never heard of and don't understand at all. For example, this." He held up a sheet of paper. "This was in Mr. Cantwell's desk. It says: *Drawn from Copa, $27,500.* And there was a deposit in his personal account for that amount. But I can't imagine what it means."

"I can tell you that," I said. "About a year ago, Cantwell bought a nightclub."

"A nightclub?" he repeated unbelievingly. He reached for his glasses, then changed his mind.

"Yes. It's called the Copacasa, and that paper probably means he drew that much money from his profits there.

"But how will I handle that in the accounts?" he said. He reached over and picked up another paper. "Now, here's a bill that I don't understand. It was in the desk, too. It's dated two months ago. It's for a month's payment in advance at some hotel. But the room was only two dollars a day and I can't imagine Mr. Cantwell staying at such a hotel."

"Maybe he wanted to get away from it—" I broke off as it penetrated. "Let me see that."

He passed it over and I looked at it. The bill was from the Emerson Hotel and it was for a room for a month at sixty dollars. There was no name on it, but I had a feeling that this might be what I was looking for.

"Maybe I can give you the answer on that, too," I said, "but first I'll check on it. I think, Mr. Patman, that you are a jewel beyond value."

"Why, thank you, Mr. March," he said, but it was obvious that he didn't know what I was talking about.

I left and drove to the address of the Emerson Hotel. It was a small, not very handsome building. I went into the small lobby. It was clean, but there was a moth-eaten look about it. There was a little old lady back of the desk, perched on a stool. She was reading a copy of one of the men's adventure magazines. She marked her place with one finger and looked up.

"Did you know," she said, "that during the last war two of our Navy men captured a whole harem of Japanese virgins? Think of that."

"It staggers my imagination," I said solemnly.

She looked over with eyes that were brighter and younger than her age would indicate. "Did you want a room?" she asked doubtfully.

"As a matter of fact, I don't," I said. "Did you have a roomer here for a while by the name of James Smith?" I was trying the name that Jimmy had given the dentist.

"Oh, yes," she said. "He was here for almost two months, the longest anyone has stayed since the days when my father owned the hotel. It was really quite a fancy hotel in those days."

"I can imagine," I said politely. "Does the hotel bear your father's name?"

"And mine. I'm Barbara Emerson." She waited expectantly.

"I'm Milo March," I provided.

"How do you do."

"How do you do," I returned. "Now, about Mr. Smith. What was he like?"

"Oh, he was very nice—except that he did drink. Not that I'm against drinking, you understand. Father always had a small drink after dinner and I do believe it made him more manly. But Mr. Smith drank rather heavily. I had a feeling that he'd had a rather unfortunate life until recently, when his friend started helping him."

"His friend?"

"Yes, that terribly nice Mr. Richards. It was he who arranged for Mr. Smith's room before he arrived. And paid one month in advance. Personally, I think Mr. Richards was sending money to Mr. Smith all the time."

"He didn't come around?" I asked.

"Mr. Richards? No, more's the pity. I think he might have been a good influence on poor Mr. Smith. But Mr. Richards was here only that one time."

I took the photograph from my pocket and held it up. "Is this Mr. Richards?"

"Of course, it is. And a very good likeness it is, too. How is dear Mr. Richards?"

"I think he's probably all right."

"Did he send you around to ask after poor Mr. Smith? I was sure that he would come around himself when it happened, but then I suppose he didn't know about it. I don't imagine the press printed anything. I never read papers. Dear father never approved. Although I did tell the police to get in touch with Mr. Richards and—"

"Wait a minute," I said. "When what happened?"

"Oh, you don't know either? My goodness! And I thought that was why you were here. I mean when poor Mr. Smith died."

"You know that he died?" I asked. "When?"

"Of course, I know. It was just last Sunday."

It was my turn to be startled. But before I could say anything she was off again.

"I did my best. I didn't have any address for that nice Mr. Richards or for Mr. Smith's other friend. But I told the police about them and urged them to try to find both men. I suppose they didn't even try very hard. The police are not what they were when I was a girl. I remember there was one who wanted to court me, but father didn't like policemen—" She broke off and peered at me. "But you're not interested in policemen, are you?"

"Not terribly so," I admitted. "What was this about Mr. Smith's other friend?

"Oh, he came to see Mr. Smith last Sunday morning. He wasn't very presentable, although he did talk like a gentleman. He was almost courtly with me. And he was carrying a large paper bag. I didn't really think Mr. Smith would see him, but he seemed very happy when he came down and saw who it was."

"Who was it?" I asked quickly while she was getting her breath.

"An old friend of Mr. Smith's—although I imagine that he was from Mr. Smith's more unfortunate days."

"I meant what was his name?"

"Oh, I don't know. He asked me to tell Mr. Smith that an old friend was here to see him. Of course, I didn't have a chance to tell him. There is no phone in Mr. Smith's room, and I wasn't going to walk up three flights. I just used this bell here"— she struck a bell that sounded more like a gong—"using the number of rings for Mr. Smith's room, and he came down."

"What happened then?"

"They went upstairs to Mr. Smith's room and I didn't see them again. Mr. Smith's friend must have left while I was in the back, refreshing myself. But do you know what must have been in that paper bag?"

"I have no idea," I admitted.

"Whiskey," she said, almost in a whisper. "There were several empty bottles in the room and one partly full. They must have been drinking all morning and I didn't know it. I suppose Mr. Smith's friend became sodden with drink and left, while Mr. Smith continued drinking. He died sometime that evening and the police said he'd had too much cheap whiskey to drink. They said they could tell he'd been drinking like that for a long time and—"

"Wait a minute," I said. This time she really had me on the ropes. "Are you telling me that James Smith died here in your hotel Sunday evening?"

"Of course. What did you think I was talking about?"

"Are you sure?"

"I found the body," she said with dignity, "when I went up to take him some fresh towels. I called the police and I talked to them after they had carried the body out. I told them to try to get in touch with Mr. Smith's two friends."

"All right," I said wearily. "I apologize. And this happened last Sunday evening? At about what time?"

"It was about five o'clock when I discovered him. It was a shock, I can tell you. Mr. Smith had been here for two months and he was almost like a member of the family—except for his drinking. But then I suppose we all must go some time or other."

"I think I will," I muttered. "Have you heard from the police since then?"

"I have not," she said indignantly. "I run a perfectly respectable hotel and the police do not bother me."

"No, I meant about Mr. Smith."

"Why should they come back about Mr. Smith? They had already taken the poor man's body. And what few possessions he had. I did think it would have been nice if they had let me know whether they were able to contact his two friends."

"I think so, too," I said weakly. "Well, thank you very much, Miss Emerson. If I ever need a good two-dollar room, I'll remember to come to you."

"Why, that's very nice of you. And I do hope, now that you know about it, you will put some flowers on poor Mr. Smith's grave."

"I'll do my best," I said. I started for the door. Then I looked back. Her finger was still paused at her reading place and her head was starting to bend over the magazine.

"And if I ever do come back, I hope you'll tell me what happened to the harem of virgins."

"If it's something proper for mixed company, I shall be glad too," she said. "Good day, Mr. Larch."

I didn't bother to correct her about my name. I went out and found the nearest bar and ordered a drink. My well-ordered case had just tumbled around my ears. Somebody had pulled the rug out from under me. Richard Cantwell had spent some time and money finding a man who superficially resembled him. He'd spent more money having the man's mouth fixed up to be an exact duplicate of his own. Then he'd put the man in a hotel and kept him there until he was ready for him. Then the man had died Sunday evening, in the hotel, several hours before the fire in Santa Monica.

I sighed, made sure that I had enough change, and went to the phone booth. I called the local police precinct. A desk sergeant answered. "Last Sunday night," I said, "a man named James Smith died in the Emerson Hotel. Your precinct answered the call. I'd like to find out about it."

"You a relative?" the sergeant asked.

"No. My name is Milo March and I'm with Intercontinental Insurance. I'm interested in the matter."

"Just a minute," he said doubtfully.

I waited and after a while another voice came on. It sounded just as bored.

"Sergeant Stevens," he said.

"My name is Milo March. I'm with Intercontinental Insurance. I've been trying to find a man named James Smith for several days, and I was just told that he died in the Emerson Hotel last Sunday and that your precinct was called. Is that right?"

"Yeah. I answered the call myself."

"Did you make any positive identification?"

"Sure. It wasn't hard. We know Jimmy of old. He was on Skid Row for a long time. He's been picked up and held until he sobered up more times than I can count. It's a wonder that cheap booze didn't kill him long ago."

"Did you find either of the two friends Miss Emerson told you about?"

"That old lady's a nut," the sergeant said. "She said find a Mr. Richards, no first name, no address. And find some other guy who was a bum, no name, no nothing. We figure that Mr. Richards was a phony name; he was probably some queer that Jimmy was shaking down, and that's why he was rich enough to move to that hotel. We'd never find Richards in a century. And neither of them would give a damn that Jimmy died."

"Did you have an autopsy performed?"

"Why an autopsy? He died from cheap liquor. Didn't need no autopsy to know that."

"Where is he buried?"

"Potter's field. Where else? The city had to pay for it. He had five bucks in his pocket."

"I see," I said. "Well, thank you, Sergeant."

"Sure," he said.

I went back to the bar and ordered another double drink. I brooded over it for a few minutes and then I began to brighten up. Maybe my thinking hadn't been as bad as I thought. I'd just made one or two little mistakes. Maybe it could still work out all right. I had more of my drink and began to feel better. I went back to the phone booth and called another number. I got a favorable answer and hung up. I left the bar and drove up to the Montecito in Hollywood. I went upstairs and Debby Vance let me in. She was still in a robe, as though she had just gotten up.

"I didn't think you meant it about that rain check," she said brightly. "Want some coffee? Reinforced."

"Sure," I said. "I can't stay long this time. I just want to ask you a couple of questions and then I have to run. But after today, I think I'll be free."

"All right," she said. She went into the kitchen and came back quickly with two cups of coffee. I tasted mine. The brandy was good and strong.

"I hear you've been seeing Pamela," she said. "Does that mean you don't suspect her anymore?"

"Not necessarily," I said. "In fact, I want to ask you a couple of questions about your vacation up in the mountains."

"Don't forget that Pamela is my friend."

"I won't. In fact, I'm not asking you to do anything wrong. If Pamela is innocent, then the truth can't hurt her. Who suggested that you go up there for a few days?"

"She did, but she is always the one who suggests it. After all, it's her place."

"Was it definite how long you were going to stay?"

"Only until we got bored. That's the way we always did it."

"Who got bored first?"

"Pamela," she said reluctantly. "She was restless Sunday night after we almost had the accident I told you about. She was still restless on Monday, and finally Tuesday morning she suddenly said we ought to go home. But that doesn't mean anything. She's always been moody like that."

"I didn't say it meant anything," I said. "How long have you known Pamela?"

"Oh, years and years. At least ten years."

"Her marriage to Cantwell was unhappy for a long time, wasn't it?"

"Yes. He was a bastard."

"I'm sure of it. How come she never took a lover when it was no good? Or did she?"

"No. I thought she should, but she wouldn't pay any attention to me. I would have if I'd been in her place."

"I bet you would have," I said with a smile. "I gather they didn't go out much, either. You mean she never had any men friends at all? I don't mean dates or an affair. I mean just a friend. She strikes me as a woman who would find it easier to be friends with a man than with a woman."

"Well, she only had one for a while. A man who was in business with her husband for a while."

"Henry Kray?"

"You know about him? She liked him when they first met. They had a lot in common. And the liking was mutual. Richard Cantwell objected, not because he thought anything was going on, but because they talked about things he wasn't interested in. Then he found a way to throw Henry Kray out of the business. Pamela thought it was very unfair."

"Did she see him after he was out of the business?"

"I think she did for a while, or at least kept in contact with him. As a matter of fact, I think he sort of went to pieces when he was thrown out, and it was Pamela who helped to pull him together. But I haven't heard her mention him in the last six months or year. Why?"

"I was just curious," I said. I finished my coffee and put down the cup. "Thanks, Debby. I have to run along now."

"Must you? You just got here. Well, if you must. But you just remember that Pamela Cantwell is a wonderful gal."

"I will," I said. "I expect to finish my work here today. But I have to stay in L.A. over the weekend. Maybe you'll have dinner with me one night."

"I'd love to," she said. "Why do you have to stay on?"

"I have to appear at an inquest next week."

"An inquest?" Her eyes suddenly widened. "Oh! You mean those two men who were shot the other night? It was an insurance investigator. Was it you?"

"Yes."

"Oh, dear," she said. "I've been in hundreds of shows where people were shot all over the place. But it wasn't real. How does it feel to kill someone?"

"It feels lousy, honey," I said. "Real lousy. I'll call you soon."

I left before she could say any more. I drove to Beverly Hills and stopped at the big white house. The maid came to the door.

"I know it's a bad hour, in the middle of the day," I said, "but would you ask Mrs. Cantwell if she can see me?"

"Of course, Mr. March," the maid said. "Will you wait in here?" She showed me into the room where I'd waited each time I'd had a date with Pamela.

I waited and in a couple of minutes the maid was back. "She's in the study upstairs. Shall I show you the way?"

"I think I remember," I said. "I'll find it."

I walked up the stairs and turned to the study. I pushed the door open and stepped inside.

She was there, looking much as she had the first time I'd seen her. She was wearing a bright red robe and looked as if she'd just gotten out of bed. She was incredibly lovely.

"Milo," she said. "This is a wonderful surprise. I thought I'd hear from you last night and then I gave up when I didn't."

"I got back too late last night," I said, "and this is the first free moment I've had today. Sorry."

"It's all right—now that you're here. Will you have a drink?"

"You know me. The answer is always yes."

She went over to the small bar and started fixing the two drinks. I looked around the room. It was the first time I'd ever really looked at it. The walls were lined with books from floor to ceiling. There was a small desk and chair. There was a beautiful Chinese screen in one corner, fanned out so that you could see only half of the window. The other chairs in the room were all comfortable and designed for contemplation. My gaze went back to her as she came across the room with the drinks. I took mine and waited for her to sit down. Then I took the chair across from her.

"To the widow Cantwell," I said, lifting my glass.

"Please," she said. "That's a horrible expression. Besides, I thought you were determined to prove that I'm not a widow."

"I wanted to talk to you," I said. "That's why I barged in like this. I want to talk about Richard Cantwell successful businessman, gay blade with the ladies, smooth operator, and gold-plated bastard—as you've said."

"All right, Milo," she said.

"Did you know he gambled?" I asked.

"No."

"Well, he did. Heavily. In the last year and a half he lost about a million dollars over the tables in Las Vegas. It was a million dollars he didn't have personally. So he started stealing from the company, from himself, to cover the losses. That didn't quite do it. So, then, on the strength of his company's business, he borrowed a half million from a bank. He set up a phony inventory to cover the money if anyone got curious."

"That's terrible," she said. "But then the thefts must be covered by insurance, aren't they?"

"The company has insurance," I said. "Also, a year ago, Richard Cantwell, who had been playing the field, met a girl who was hard to get. He even bought a nightclub to get her, and that didn't work. But finally he did get her—when she thought she loved him. And by that time I think he believed he loved her. But he was in a bad way. He had a successful business from which he had stolen a million dollars. Maybe it was his own money, but if nothing else, the Internal Revenue boys would view the whole thing with jaundiced eyes. He also had treated his wife very badly, and she certainly wouldn't let him off easy if he went to her and suddenly said he wanted a divorce."

"You mean he wanted to marry the girl?"

"I think he did. So he had a bright idea. He stole another five hundred thousand dollars from his business. Then he planned to have one of his houses burned down and it would seem that he and his wife had perished in the fire. That would mean one million three hundred thousand dollars. Granting that he might have to give a half million dollars to Harry Manfred for arranging the fire, it would still leave him with a tidy sum to start a new life with a new love somewhere."

"I don't understand," she said. "How would he get the money?"

"I don't know," I admitted. "I've checked the foundation and I don't think they were involved. But your husband must have had an idea. Or maybe he just trusted in the fact that he believed he always got what he wanted. In the meantime, he still had a half million in cash to hold him while he waited for the insurance money."

"But how was he going to make people believe that he had died in the fire?"

"He went to Skid Row, near his office, and found a bum who was more or less like him physically. I don't know what story he used, but he got the bum to have his teeth fixed so that they would match his. The plan was that the bum and Richard Cantwell's wife would die in the fire. It was a nice plan—but not too original."

"So that's what happened?" she said. She shuddered. "But how did the girl get there instead of me?"

"A few things went wrong with his plan," I said. "For one thing, Richard Cantwell's wife found out what was going on. I don't know exactly how. Maybe she found his money. He had almost seven hundred thousand dollars in cash, and he had to keep it somewhere. He probably hid it in the house. Maybe she found it and maybe she noticed a few other peculiar things. I doubt if she figured it out all by herself. She had a friend—a very close friend—who had once worked with Richard Cantwell. He knew him very well—and hated him. He probably guessed what the plan was, and the two of them decided to let Cantwell work out his idea up to a point, and then they would make certain changes in it."

I paused but she didn't say anything. She just stared at me, her face pale and frozen.

"When this friend was thrown out by Cantwell," I continued, "I think he ended up on Skid Row. He was more or less rescued from that by Richard Cantwell's wife. She supported him for the next few years. When they discovered Cantwell's plan, they saw their chance to have a life together and do it with plenty of money. And they probably saw an ironic justice in the fact that Richard Cantwell and his mistress would die in the fire, instead of Cantwell's wife and some nameless bum from Skid Row.

"Richard Cantwell had his plan set for Tuesday night. He was going to meet his wife at the Santa Monica house when she came back from vacation. Maybe he thought he'd convinced her that they would start all over again. He would have the bum there the same night. He probably intended to see that they were both knocked out in some fashion, then he'd leave and let his hired arsonists do their work. He'd booked air passage to Las Vegas for the next morning under a different name. I'm not sure why Las Vegas—he certainly couldn't go near the tables—but it might have been because there's so much traffic in and out of Las Vegas that he thought it would be easy to vanish from there.

"But Cantwell didn't know that his wife and former partner were also busy with their own plans. Somehow they found out who the arsonist was that Cantwell had hired. They approached him and outbid Cantwell, so he agreed to work for them. They had also discovered that Cantwell and his mistress were spending a lot of time at the Santa Monica house and were pretty certain they would be there over the weekend—especially since Cantwell's wife would be in the mountains for the weekend. So that part was ready.

"To go back for a minute, when they first got the idea that Cantwell was planning something, I think they realized that he would have to provide a double to be found in the fire. The wife's friend was probably the one to realize that the logical place for a double to be found was on Skid Row—that haven for nameless and friendless men so near Cantwell's offices. So he went back to Skid Row and kept a silent and unseen watch. When Cantwell did go there to find his man, the friend soon found out about it. He also found out that Cantwell took the bum to a dentist to have his teeth fixed, and stayed around until he learned where Cantwell took the bum. Then he came back to his normal life.

"They arranged with Harry Manfred to do his torch job on Sunday night. The wife was safely away in the country with a woman who could swear she was there all the time. They even had a near accident—which I suspect was arranged by the friend—so it might look as if her husband had tried to kill her. Everything went off as planned.

"Then an insurance investigator showed up. They realized that he might stumble onto something that would make him suspicious of Cantwell, and that if he did, then he, too, might end up on Skid Row looking for that double. So the friend let his beard grow and once again started playing his role down there. Sure enough, I did show up and he was just helpful enough to let me find out that Cantwell had picked up a bum and had his teeth fixed to match Cantwell's. But he didn't help me find out where the bum had gone. He didn't want me to find that out because he had visited the bum on Sunday, in his role as a fellow bum, and gotten drunk with him. But there was poison in the double's liquor and he conveniently vanished from the scene—just as he would have if Cantwell's scheme had gone through.

"Pretty, isn't it? There is a villain, but it's not Cantwell. My insurance company and I were to believe that he'd planned to kill his wife and a nameless man so he could collect the insurance, but that something had gone wrong and he'd failed to kill the wife. Since she was not part of the scheme, we can't claim that she was party to the fraud, and at the very least she'll collect the fire insurance. And she might with luck collect the half million on her husband. In the meantime, she has about seven hundred thousand dollars for pin money— the dough her husband took. The insurance company prob- ably won't make good the stolen money, but she'll still be sitting pretty with between one million and one and a half million dollars. She has to pay Harry Manfred six hundred thousand, but she has seven hundred thousand left on which there will be no taxes. And she'll still have a successful busi- ness, which her lover can run. Sometime later they can even get married.

"You know, it was a clever plan, honey. But not clever

enough. There were holes in it. I'll admit that I found most of them at the last minute and by accident, but the point is that I did find them."

She finally found her voice. "What are you talking about?" she asked.

"You know," I said wearily. "I think you and your friend also decided that you should be friendly with me so that you might be able to learn what I was doing. You entered into that role so enthusiastically that you even went to bed with me—did you tell him that? Did you tell him all the details? Or did you try to make him believe that you only pretended to enjoy yourself?"

Her face had gone paper white. She glanced nervously around the room. She opened her mouth to speak, but no sound came out.

"I think," I said, "that my barroom friend Hank—Henry Kray—is waiting back of that screen. Otherwise you would have shown more affection when I first came in. So why not invite him out?"

He came around the screen. He was clean-shaven and well dressed. There was a gun in his hand. He gave her a brief venomous glance, then turned his full attention to me. "My benefactor," he said bitterly. "He who 'came like water, and like wind' will go."

"I'm glad to see that you're in character," I told him. "I don't know what I would have done if you hadn't recited something from Omar. But I had expected 'The Flower that once has blown for ever dies.' "

"There's still time," he said grimly.

"You know something else," I said. "That seven hundred thousand dollars you have isn't worth a dime."

"What do you mean?"

"It's mostly stolen money, and the bank has the serial numbers of all the bills. You can't spend them without their being identified as the money Richard Cantwell stole from his company and withdrew from his personal account."

He glanced at her briefly again. "I told you he was dangerous. But he seems to have come here first. We can take care of it."

"How?" she asked, and she sounded close to tears.

"We can turn him over to Manfred. He's getting enough money. Or I can take care of him myself. I might like that."

"That's the trouble with amateurs," I said. "They never know when to quit. Well, at least let me have another drink before I die." I held my glass out.

Automatically, like the well-bred hostess, she got up and came over to get my glass. As she took it from me, she was partly in between us.

"Pamela," he said desperately.

But it was too late. I let my hand go with the glass and shoved her as hard as I could. She went staggering back into him. I didn't wait to see the results. I hit the floor, rolling, pulling my gun from its holster. I ended up on my belly, facing him.

He was off balance and I had plenty of time. I took careful aim and put a bullet through his kneecap. He screamed once and flopped on the floor. The gun skidded away from his nerveless fingers. I got up and went over to pick up his gun.

I looked down at him. He was crying with pain. His trouser leg was already dark with blood.

Suddenly she was pulling at me. "Do something! He's bleeding. Oh, Milo, he might bleed to death!"

"Let him," I said.

"No," she said. It was almost a scream. "Don't let him die. I'll do anything you say."

"No, Pamela," he said between clenched teeth, but she wasn't listening.

"I'll tell you what I'll do," I said. "I'll call the police. When they get here, you tell them how it was. Then they can take him to the hospital."

"Yes, yes," she said. "I'll do anything. Just don't let him die. I love him."

I looked to see if he was going to protest again, but he'd fainted. I went over and picked up the phone. I called the police department and asked for Lieutenant Arnold.

"Milo March," I said when he came on. "Are you busy?"

"Why?"

"If you'd care to drive out to the Cantwell house, you can wrap up the case."

"You found Cantwell?"

"No," I said. "I was wrong about that. It was Cantwell in the fire. Put there by his wife and her lover. The lover has a bullet hole through his right knee. She's anxious for you to get here quickly, so she can tell you all about it and you'll get him to a doctor."

"I'll be right there," he said and hung up.

TEN

Lieutenant Arnold was there in less than twenty minutes. He listened while Pamela Cantwell sobbed out her story. It was pretty much as I'd outlined it. A police stenographer was taking it down as she talked. When she'd finished, I filled in the few things she'd left out. In the meantime, a policeman had administered first aid to Hank. Then the Lieutenant took them away. I promised I'd be in Monday to make my statement formally. I left, too. I was tired.

I parked the car beside the hotel and headed for my bungalow. I was almost there when I saw there were lights inside. I slowed up and approached the windows instead of the door. I finally found one where the curtains weren't completely closed. I shifted around, peering in. Then I saw a mass of red hair and a bare shoulder. I didn't need to see more. It could be only one person. Torchy—and in pretty much the same condition as when I'd first seen her.

I retreated to the main building of the hotel and called the police again. I asked for Lieutenant Arnold. He was there.

"What the hell do you want now?" he demanded. "I'm just trying to clean up the mess you handed me before."

"Did she sign her statement?"

"Yeah. Is that the only reason you called?"

"No. I've got another one for you. If you want to come to my hotel to pick her up."

"Her?"

"Her. But she was the torch on the job. For Harry Manfred. I think she's ready to talk. Between her and Pamela Cantwell, you can really tie up Harry Manfred, and that ought to be a feather in your cap."

"I'll have to pick up somebody from the Santa Monica Police," he said, "but I'll be there as soon as I can."

I went back to the bungalow and unlocked the door. I stepped inside. Torchy was there on the couch. *Sans* clothing. Only this time there wasn't a gun in her hand. There was only a drink.

"Hello," I said, closing the door behind me. "I think I've seen you somewhere before."

"Milo," she said, "can I stay here tonight? I'm afraid. If you let me stay, I'll do what you want me to in the morning. I'll tell all about Harry Manfred. But if I don't stay here, I'm afraid he'll have me killed. And we can have our date."

"It's too late, Torchy," I said gently. "The whole thing has been blown wide open. Maybe you can help yourself by talking, but it's too late to be the star."

"Please," she said.

"Besides, I'm tired of everybody making with my room like it was Penn Station. And I'm tired of everybody wanting to use me as a clay pigeon. And I'm just tired." She just stared at me, her eyes big and round.

"You'll be safe," I said. "Manfred won't be able to get to you. Now, put on your clothes."

She got up, wordlessly, and obeyed. When she was dressed she sat down, almost primly, and waited. I smoked a cigarette and waited with her. I didn't feel like talking.

Lieutenant Arnold made it in forty minutes, which was pretty good. There was a big, burly Santa Monica cop with him. I introduced them to Torchy and explained her role in the case. She just nodded when he looked at her. Then they started to take her away. Lieutenant Arnold stopped at the door and looked back at me.

"I suppose I should thank you," he said sourly.

"Not at all," I told him. "It's all yours and you can take all the credit. I'll get my thanks from my company—in the form of a check, which is the only thanks I like. Forget it."

"When are you planning on leaving, March?"

"Right after the inquest."

"Good," he said. "You're too quick with a trigger, March. I don't like people like that in my jurisdiction. The next time you might shoot the wrong one."

"You mean like some trigger-happy cop?" I asked. "Look, Lieutenant, I'm tired. I didn't solve your case; I solved my case. I don't give a damn about you or your cases. I turned what I found over to you because these people need to be reckoned with—legally. If you were up the creek without a paddle, I wouldn't pull you out, even if you were in over your badge. Good-bye, Lieutenant."
He glared at me, but he left without saying anything more.

I was glad to see him go. It was still early evening, for it had gotten dark just before I reached the hotel, but I was tired. I took off my coat and tie and poured myself a drink. There were a couple of things I wanted to do.

I picked up the phone and asked the hotel operator to get me the Shamrock bar in Los Angeles. A few minutes later, a man answered.

"Is this the bartender?" I asked.

"Yeah."

"This is the man who gave you a hundred dollars," I said. "Do you remember?"

"Yeah, but I don't have anything for you yet."

"I know. I don't need it now. So take fifty dollars and buy drinks for the bar until it's gone. Put the other fifty in your pocket."

"Okay," he said.

He wasn't much of a conversationalist, but that suited me at the moment. I said good-bye and hung up. Then I put through a call to Martin Raymond at his home in New York. He was there.

"Milo, boy," he said when he heard my voice, "what's up?"

"I just saved you a few million dollars," I said, "and I hope you appreciate it."

"You broke the case?"

"In a million pieces. I'll give you the details tomorrow or someday, but I thought you'd sleep better if you knew. You won't have to pay any of the insurance, and I also got Harry Manfred for you. The way I figure it, it took five days, which means that it cost you only five hundred dollars plus expenses."

"Milo," he said, "I had a talk with the Board of Directors this afternoon. We have already decided that if you broke this one you'd get a bonus of ten thousand dollars."

"I like the way you talk," I said.

"The check will be ready for you when you get back. You're taking the plane tomorrow?"

"No. I have to stay for an inquest And I expect to stay on the expense account. I have two lovely phone numbers for the weekend, one Occidental and the other Oriental. I'll see you next week."

"Okay, Milo."

"One more thing," I said. "There's a dentist out here who's been some help. As a matter of fact his testimony will be pretty important. His practice isn't so good and he's looking for a job. Can Intercontinental use a dentist?"

"Maybe. Tell him to go see the local office. I'll advise them that he's coming. What's his name?"

"Phillips."

"All right. Sorry, I have to run now. My wife and I are having a bridge party tonight."

"Redouble somebody for me," I said, "just for the hell of it. Good night, Martin."

I hung up and poured myself another drink, a stiff one. Then I went to bed despite the fact that it was only dinnertime. I fell asleep immediately and dreamed about a redhead and a blonde. Both were in iron cages and I couldn't get to them. Which was pretty accurate for a dream.

ABOUT THE AUTHOR

Kendell Foster Crossen
(1910–1981), the only child
of Samuel Richard Cros-
sen and Clo Foster Cros-
sen, was born on a farm
outside Albany in Athens
County, Ohio—a village of
some 550 souls in the year
of this birth. His ancestors
on his mother's side include
the 19th-century songwriter
Stephen Collins Foster
("Oh! Susanna"); William

Allen, founder of Allentown, Pennsylvania; and Ebenezer
Foster, one of the Minute Men who sprang to arms at the
Lexington alarm in April 1775.

Ken went to Rio Grande College on a football scholarship
but stayed only one year. "When I was fairly young, I developed the disgusting habit of reading," says Milo March,
and it seems Ken Crossen, too, preferred self-education.
He loved literature and poetry; favorite authors included
Christopher Marlowe and Robert Service. He also enjoyed
participant sports and was a semi-pro fighter in the heavy-

weight class. He became a practicing magician and had a passion for chess.

After college Ken wrote several one-act plays that were produced in a small Cleveland theater. He worked in steel mills and Fisher Body plants. Then he was employed as an insurance investigator, or "claims adjuster," in Cleveland. But he left the job and returned to the theater, now as a performer: a tumbling clown in the Tom Mix Circus; a comic and carnival barker for a tent show, and an actor in a medicine show.

In 1935, Ken hitchhiked to New York City with a typewriter under his arm, and found work with the WPA Writers' Project, covering cricket for the *New York City Guidebook*. In 1936, he was hired by the Munsey Publishing Company as associate editor of the popular *Detective Fiction Weekly*. The company asked him to come up with a character to compete with The Shadow, and thus was born a unique superhero of pulps, comic books, and radio—The Green Lama, an American mystic trained in Tibetan Buddhism.

Crossen sold his first story, "The Aaron Burr Murder Case," to *Detective Fiction Weekly* in September 1939, but says he didn't begin to make a living from writing till 1941. He tried his hand at publishing true crime magazines, comics, and a picture magazine, without great success, so he set out for Hollywood. From his typewriter flowed hundreds of stories, short novels for magazines, scripts radio, television, and film, nonfiction articles. He delved into science fiction in the 1950s, starting with "Restricted Clientele" (February 1951). His dystopian novels *Year of Consent* and *The Rest Must Die* also appeared in this decade.

In the course of his career Ken Crossen acquired six pseud-onyms: Richard Foster, Bennett Barlay, Kent Richards, Clay Richards, Christopher Monig, and M.E. Chaber. The variety was necessary because different publishers wanted to reserve specific bylines for their own publications. Ken based "M.E. Chaber" on the Hebrew word for "author," *mechaber*.

In the early '50s, as M.E. Chaber, Crossen began to write a series of full-length mystery/espionage novels featuring Milo March, an insurance investigator. The first, *Hangman's Harvest,* was published in 1952. In all, there are twenty-two Milo March novels. One, *The Man Inside,* was made into a British film starring Jack Palance.

Most of Ken's characters were private detectives, and Milo was the most popular. Paperback Library reissued twenty-five Crossen titles in 1970–1971, with covers by Robert McGin-nis. Twenty were Milo March novels, four featured an insur-ance investigator named Brian Brett, and one was about CIA agent Kim Locke.

Crossen excelled at producing well-plotted entertainment with fast-moving action. His research skills were a strong asset, back when research meant long hours searching library microfilms and poring over street maps and hotel floorplans. His imagination took him to many international hot spots, although he himself never traveled abroad. Like Milo March, he hated flying ("When you've seen one cloud, you've seen them all").

Ken Crossen was married four times. With his first wife he had three children (Stephen, Karen, Kendra) and with his second a son (David). He lived in New York, Florida, Southern California, Nevada, and other parts of the country. Milo March moves from Denver to New York City after five books of the series, with an apartment on Perry Street in Greenwich Village; that's where Ken lived, too. His and Milo's favorite watering hole was the Blue Mill Tavern, a short walk from the apartment.

Ken Crossen was a combination of many of the traits of his different male characters: tough, adventuresome, with a taste for gin and shapely women. But perhaps the best observation was made in an obituary written by sci-fi writer Avram Davidson, who described Ken as a fundamentally gentle person who had been buffeted by many winds.